jFic

Fenner, Phyllis R.
Desperate moments >< journeys.
NAPOLEON PUBLIC LIBRARY

3 2930 99029230 5

Despe

STORIES
AND HU

Desperate Moments

STORIES OF ESCAPES AND HURRIED JOURNEYS SELECTED BY
PHYLLIS R. FENNER
illustrated by Charles Geer

Faced with unbearable pressure, insurmountable odds, or inescapable danger, the human spirit responds with subtle wit and cunning plus a fund of courage and stamina almost superhuman.

These stories tell of that wit and that courage. There is a boy who rides seven hundred miles, almost without rest or food, to save his father's ranch; a captive woman who runs away from a band of hostile Indians, then travels days on end through unbroken wilderness as, with her baby, she struggles toward the settlements and safety; there is Cue, born in a field-hand's cabin, who, because of the freedom he feels in his heart, takes the perilous Underground Railroad to the North; there is a judge who suddenly finds himself on the wrong side of the law; and a man who must find a way to escape the sheriff's fatal trap to win the woman he loves.

Truman Capote, Conrad Richter, Paul Gallico, and Stephen Vincent Benét are among the ten authors represented in this collection of varied adventures compiled by an experienced and esteemed anthologist.

STORIES OF ESCAPES AND HURRIED JOURNEYS

illustrated by Charles Geer

Desperate Moments

SELECTED BY

PHYLLIS R. FENNER

William Morrow and Company | New York

71- 3381

Copyright © 1971 by Phyllis R. Fenner

Grateful acknowledgment is made for permission to reprint the following:
"Sacrifice Spurs," by Carl Henry Rathjen. Copyright 1955 by The Boy
Scouts of America. Reprinted by permission of the author and Larry Sternig
Literary Agency.
"Enemy Agent," by Thomas Walsh. Copyright 1943 by The Curtis Pub-
lishing Company. Reprinted by permission of *The Saturday Evening Post.*
"The Iron Lady," by Conrad Richter. Copyright © 1957 by The Curtis
Publishing Company. Reprinted by permission of Paul R. Reynolds, Inc.,
599 Fifth Ave., New York, N.Y. 10017.
"No Rescue," by James Norman. Copyright © 1954 by The Curtis Pub-
lishing Company. Reprinted by permission of *The Saturday Evening Post.*
"Freedom's a Hard Bought Thing," by Stephen Vincent Benét. Copyright
1940 by The Curtis Publishing Company. Reprinted by permission of
Brandt & Brandt.
"The White Mustang," by Jack Schaefer. Copyright 1966 by Jack Schaefer.
Originally appeared in *Boys' Life,* published by The Boy Scouts of America.
Reprinted by permission of the Harold Matson Company, Inc.
"A Diamond Guitar," by Truman Capote. Copyright 1950 by Truman
Capote. Reprinted from *Selected Writings of Truman Capote* by permission
of Random House, Inc.
"Rock River Fugitive," by Mary Roberts Rinehart. Reprinted by permission
of Frederick R. Rinehart.
"Death Trap," by Paul Gallico. Copyright 1955 by The Curtis Publishing
Company. Reprinted from *Further Confessions of a Story Writer* by per-
mission of Doubleday & Company, Inc. (First published in *The Saturday
Evening Post* under the title "Love Is a Gimmick.")
"The Letter of the Law," by Don Knowlton. Copyright © 1962 by Davis
Publications, Inc. First published in *Ellery Queen's Mystery Magazine.* Re-
printed by permission of the author.

All rights reserved. No part of this book may be reproduced or utilized in
any form or by any means, electronic or mechanical, including photocopy-
ing, recording or by any information storage and retrieval system, without
permission in writing from the Publisher. Inquiries should be addressed to
William Morrow and Company, Inc., 105 Madison Ave., New York,
N.Y. 10016.
Printed in the United States of America.

Library of Congress Catalog Card Number 77-155496

1 2 3 4 5 75 74 73 72 71

jFic
F

This book is for Esther,
who has had her desperate moments.

71-3381

Contents

Desperate Moments

STORIES OF ESCAPES AND HURRIED JOURNEYS

Liberty

Next to love of life the love of liberty appears to be the strongest feeling in man. Perhaps for this reason stories of pursuit and escape make the most exciting adventure tales.

Every escape is subject to chance. There is always something unforeseen, something unknown to overcome. In order to escape from prison or bondage, men have scaled the absolute heights of human courage and ingenuity. They have made use of wooden horses and tunnels, gone through impassable jungles, endured exhaustion and starvation. Both history and fiction are full of instances where a human being has achieved freedom in a miraculous manner.   P. F.

Sacrifice Spurs

CARL HENRY RATHJEN

Dave Remy spotted the silver spurs in a Sacramento store window that California dawn of February 23, 1855, as he and old Jep Frey, his dad's ranch foreman, hurried down crowded K Street.

"Jep, look!" He pointed as gold miners and townspeople jostled by on their way to the riverfront. Jep Frey turned his gray head from the street jammed with stagecoaches waiting the arrival of the steamboat from Frisco.

"Think you've earned them?" he asked.

Dave tugged his gaze from the spurs. Beauties. Just the kind that his dad, recovering from a horse's kick, had said he could buy if he proved himself man enough to get a good price for cattle in Sacramento.

"Yesterday," Dave began defensively, "you said that $12,500 in gold wasn't bad at all in these hard times."

Then he saw the twinkle in Jep's eyes. He started eagerly toward the store, but Jep grabbed his arm. "You can buy spurs anytime. It ain't every day we get to town to see the steamboat arrive from the big city. And look at all them stagecoaches waiting to gallop to Hangtown, Auburn, Marysville, everywhere in the Mother Lode Country."

"You look," said Dave, his excited eyes on those spurs again. "I'll find you down on the levee."

But Jep hung on to his arm as the crowd shouldered by. "Better give me that deposit certificate, son. Your pa's countin' heavy on that gold. And this is the kind of a crowd that pickpockets like."

The word *son* stung a bit. Dave spoke up. "I was old enough to sell those cattle, Jep. Guess I'm man enough to take care of that gold certificate—and this, too." Dave patted the bulge of his wallet, which had the five hundred dollars his father had said to bring home. "Besides, the certificate can't be cashed by anyone except me or Dad. His gold is safe in the bank."

Jep studied him, and then smiled. "See you down at the levee then—man-size spurs and all."

Dave dashed into the store. He strapped on the silver spurs, though it would be a few hours before he, Jep, and the ranch hands got their horses from the livery stable and started home. As he proudly jingled out on K Street again, a boisterous group of miners jostled him. He quickly felt for the wallet's reassuring bulge.

He thought of Jep's warning. He'd heard stories too about picking pockets. The hard times tempted people to be light-fingered. Gold miners were up against it because this winter's scant rainfall had shut down placer operations. As a result, San Francisco business slumped. The East had had a hard winter too. So had his dad. But that gold deposit certificate was a windfall that would hold things together.

Dave suddenly didn't like the idea of getting into the thick of the riverfront crowd to look for Jep. Someone, smart enough to steal that certificate from him, might be clever enough to get it honored at the bank. His dad would surely lose the ranch then. So, reluctantly turning his back on the arriving steamboat, he strolled up K Street like a man too busy and important to be interested in ordinary excitements —until he reached Bremond's restaurant. Hey, he hadn't had breakfast yet!

Gravely, as befitted a man who had earned his spurs and would someday own one of the largest ranches in the Sacramento Valley, he entered and ordered two stacks of flapjacks with sausages, a side order of bacon and eggs, fresh rolls and jam, coffee, two wedges of pie, and a bottle of root juice.

With that man-sized meal straining his belt, he jingled outside. Everyone was now hurrying from the riverfront toward a crowd farther uptown. Dave wondered what the new excitement was about.

Then hard fingers bit into his arm. Jep Frey glared at him. "Where in blazes have you been? I've looked all over for you! What're you doing *standing* here?"

"I've been having breakfast," Dave began, puzzled.

"Spurs! Breakfast!" snapped Jep Frey. "Ain't you heard there's a run on the bank before it closes its doors?"

"The Adams Bank?" Dave gasped.

"What else would I be worried about?" Jep retorted, yanking him out of his daze. "If you'd been at the levee, you'd have heard that the panic back East hit Frisco yesterday. It started a run, everybody running to the bank, all at the same time, and drawin' out their money. All the Frisco banks are closed. The Adams home office there has failed, closed forever. And it's anybody's guess how long the Sacramento branch can stay open and pay out. . . ."

Dave heard no more as he dashed ahead. His dad, the ranch, everything depended on that $12,000 gold deposit. With Jep shoving behind him, he fought through the crowd into the bank. He thrust the deposit certificate at a harried clerk, caught at the lapels by Jep's big fist.

"I can't!" yelled the clerk. "Wait your turn in line!"

The crowd agreed angrily. A miner called to Dave, "You should have got here half an hour ago, kid."

A half hour ago he'd been swaggering with his new spurs into Bremond's. Dave couldn't look at Jep as they sought the end of the line. Outside. Down the street. Around the corner. Dave's heart sank clear down to those danged spurs.

"We'll be all day reaching the window," he groaned.

"If the bank's got any money or gold left by then." Jep glowered.

Dave felt like giving up that man-sized breakfast. He stared at the certificate, now just an empty promise to pay.

"Jep! I've still got a chance! This is payable at any branch of the Adams Bank. There won't be a run like this in Hangtown, Auburn, anywhere in the Mother Lode country. Not yet anyway."

"The telegraph already flashed the bad news from here

all over California," Jep growled. "Wait a minute!" He squinted. "There's not a chance in California. But, Dave, there isn't a telegraph line to Portland, Oregon! They won't know up there! So if we catch the ship *Columbia* sailing from Frisco this afternoon. . . ."

Dave turned eagerly toward the riverfront. "That wad of five hundred will take care of our passage," he agreed, patting his wallet. Then he stopped short. "Jep! The *Columbia* will carry the bad news with us! And the Portland branch will refuse to honor the certificate when they hear how everything's closed down here!"

Jep looked suddenly haggard, then spoke through his teeth. "I hope you're satisfied with the price you paid for those spurs. Twelve thousand in gold *and* your dad's ranch!"

Dave blinked down at the silver spurs. Sacrifice spurs! They'd made him feel so grown-up, ready to take his place beside his father riding about the ranch. Riding. . . . "Jep, these spurs may save everything yet."

Jep laughed harshly. "If you mean what I think. . . ."

"I'll beat the *Columbia* by *riding* to Portland."

"You're crazy!" Jep exploded. "It's a good seven hundred miles!"

"You've called me a riding fool," Dave argued. "You've taught me how to ride, toughened me up."

"Not for seven hundred miles over mountains against time. You'd have to ride day and night for a week—*if* you could stay in the saddle that long."

"I've got to," Dave cut in. "It's my only chance."

"It's throwing the chance away! Take the *Columbia,* son. When she docks in Portland, we'll get to the bank ahead of the bad news and. . . ."

"It'll be shouted ashore before we can get off her," Dave insisted. "Then what?"

"It's a better try than having you fold up somewhere in the mountains. You ain't made of iron. Gimme that deposit certificate. *I'm* taking the *Columbia!*"

They turned as a steamboat whistle sounded. Then Dave raced for the riverfront. Jep panted after him.

"Now you're showin' sense, son. We'll. . . ."

Dave sprinted as he saw a stern-wheeler edging away from the wharf. Jep followed behind him.

"Not that boat, you fool! She's goin' upriver!"

Dave leaped wildly across water. His spurs gouged planking as a deckhand caught him. He turned quickly and called to Jep on the receding wharf, "I know it. I'll be waiting with the gold when the *Columbia* docks in Portland."

Jep gave him a hard look, then vanished into the crowd.

Dave paced as the stern-wheeler thrashed its tortuous way up the Sacramento River. What had he jumped into with those blamed spurs? Seven hundred hard-riding miles. But the more he miserably thought about his pop's losing the ranch the more he knew he had made the only possible decision. Get to Portland *before,* not with, the bad news. He prayed that the *Columbia* was as slow as this creaking riverboat.

At last the old tub swung into Knight's Landing, forty-two miles upriver from Sacramento. Dave jumped to the wharf and cut short the greeting from old man Knight, his father's friend. "I need a good *fast* horse, Mr. Knight. Will you sell me one?"

"You can't buy a horse from me, son." Dave turned away

angrily. A fine friend! "But take my best mount at the head of the wharf."

"Thanks." Dave grinned over his shoulder. Excited, he startled the drowsing bay stallion. It reared into life, fighting his efforts to mount. Swinging up, he pricked it with a spur. The lunging stallion nearly threw him. His cheeks burned as everyone stared. Nice way to start the long ride to Portland, forgetting all the horsemanship Jep had taught him!

He calmed himself, then the horse, walking it a quarter mile till it became accustomed to his weight. Then a quarter mile of trotting. Another galloping. Trot again. Walk. Trot. Gallop again with the other forefoot leading this time. Give the horse a chance to stay fresh longer, keep from getting leg-weary.

Riding north through the hot, dry Sacramento Valley he glanced eastward toward the High Sierra draped with snow. Their ranch nestled over there in the foothills, its entire future dependent on a nest egg of gold in Portland, nearly seven hundred miles away. Dave tugged down his hat brim as he spurred the stallion ahead.

Late that afternoon he rode the weary horse up to a ranch house huddling under towering eucalyptus trees. A young man and a woman, holding a baby, came out as he dismounted, patting the stallion.

"Sir," Dave requested, "will you sell me a horse and return this one to Mr. Knight down the valley?"

"Reckon I can," said the man. "But if you've ridden all the way from Knight's you'd better set awhile."

"Just in time for supper." The young woman smiled.

Dave realized he hadn't eaten all day. Not since Bremond's!

"Thanks, but I haven't the time. Now about that horse, sir."

After he saddled up while explaining his haste, the young woman handed him a package of food to take along. "I'll pray that you make it to Portland in time," she said.

As he rode away, he heard her speak to her husband. "I used to envy people who had money in the bank."

He traveled fast until darkness blotted out everything but the stars. He let the horse have its head and kept his eye on the North Star . . . until it exploded into a thousand stars when the limb of a tree smashed him in the face. He clung to the saddle, fighting dizziness. He ought to wait for daylight to travel in this strange country. But the *Columbia* would steam north all night. He squinted into the darkness and urged the horse onward.

At dawn he roused a fat, grumpy liveryman in Red Bluff and made a deal to trade horses. Asking the man to call him in an hour, he burrowed into a pile of hay. He dreamed he was crawling toward a pile of gold, but someone hauled him back by the shoulder. He fought desperately.

"Easy, kid," a voice said. He opened his eyes and saw the liveryman bending over him. "Hour's up." The man grinned.

Dave stumbled to his horse, put his foot in the stirrup, and felt no bulge in his hip pocket. He whirled.

"Where's my wallet?" he demanded, advancing. The man's hand dropped toward a gun. Dave dove, clamping on the wrist. The heavy liveryman swung him off his feet and piled onto him. Dave felt himself being pinned down. He got a leg clear, lifted it, then brought it down hard, driving a silver spur into the man's rump. The liveryman howled. Dave wriggled free, smashed him in the face, and got the gun.

"All right, all right," the man yelled. "Here!"

Dave quickly checked the wad in his wallet and, most important of all, the deposit certificate. Mounting, he tossed the gun in the hayloft and rode away.

The sun climbed to the noon sky and hurled its heat into the Sacramento Valley. Mountains shimmered. Dust devils swirled. Dave's eyes smarted with sweat. Twenty-four hours since he'd left Knight's Landing. It seemed like twenty-four years. But here he was, still in this blasted valley, still in California. And the livery stable plug lathering out under him. How had he ever imagined he could make it to Portland in time to save his dad's ranch?

He goaded the wheezing nag to a ranch just south of Redding and bought a chunky pinto that the foreman said would "take the mountains ahead like they was the flats." That night, in black mountains hulking below snowcapped Mount Shasta, he wished he had bought a coat along with the pinto. The moon hung like ice among brittle stars. Trees cracked in the sharp coldness. He ran beside his trotting horse in an effort to warm up. Back in the saddle he fought drowsiness.

He woke up, half frozen, outside a cabin above a rushing river as a little gray-headed lady tried to get him out of the saddle. He tumbled off numbly, and she steadied him into a kitchen warm with the odor of freshly baked bread. As he thawed out by the stove, he glanced out the window down toward the river where two men, probably her husband and son, were fishing.

"W-what r-river is th-that?"

"The Sacramento, son."

He groaned. Just how long was that river? Was he ever going to get out of California and into Oregon? He asked about getting a horse.

"We'll talk about that later," she said, giving him a motherly smile. "You have some breakfast first, and then some rest. You're all tuckered out."

"I had my sleep on the horse," Dave replied, still shivering and trying not to think about a soft bed and warm blankets. She persisted, but tired as he was he wouldn't give in. Too risky. She was a nice old lady who'd think she was doing him a favor to let him sleep on and on and on—while somewhere off the coast the *Columbia* steamed northward for Portland.

"Then at least," she said finally, "you'll let me fix you a man-sized breakfast."

The cool mountains made for fast riding all that day. By nightfall he'd dropped into the valley north of Weed and hoped to keep up the good pace in flat country. Then wind blasted out of the darkness. The notorious wind of that area that could rip a farmer's seed out of the soil. Wind that could almost lift a man from the saddle and tear him away from a desperately needed crop of gold waiting in Portland. A wind that kept him continually battling the horse, which wanted to turn tail and drift in the wrong direction.

Feeling battered and beaten from the blustering night, he rode on, and along toward noon of that third day he swayed into Yreka, still in California, but only twenty miles south of the Oregon border. He wanted to keep pushing, but what if he fell asleep in the saddle again and became lost in the mountains. He'd been lucky last night. So, after trading horses and ordering the new one to be saddled and ready to go in an hour, he reluctantly got a room in a hotel.

The bored desk clerk nodded vaguely when Dave asked to be called later. He'd better wake himself up. But how?

He was so exhausted he'd fall in too deep for his inner senses to pull him out before precious time had been lost.

He stared about the shabby room. A decrepit bed. A rickety chair. The usual pitcher of water and basin. Battered bureau with cracked mirror. A candle in a bottle. Yawning, he saw the cord from the window shade. An inch or so from the top of the candle he cut a notch clear into the wick. Fastening the cord to the mirror, he strung it through the notch, touching the wick, and tied the other end to the handle of the pitcher balanced precariously on the edge of the bureau and only prevented from tipping by the cord.

Lighting the candle, he spread blankets and pillow on the floor below the bureau and plunged into darkness—until the candle flame burned down to the cord and severed it. A flood of water doused his head. The pitcher bounded off his chest. He sat up sputtering and reached for his boots . . . and those silver spurs.

North of Yreka the road climbed, higher and higher into the Siskiyou Mountains while the sun dropped lower and lower. In the evening hush of the darkening mountains he was giving his horse a walking breather when he heard hoofs furiously pounding back around the last bend. At least a dozen or more horses. He frowned uneasily. Outlaws? A posse? A bunch out for a hilarious time? He couldn't mix in anything that might delay him.

He spurred into a shadowy clump of brush a moment before a sheriff's posse rounded the bend. As they charged by the sheriff raised his arm. They hauled horses back on haunches just up the road.

"Don't see his tracks no more, boys. Head back and watch for where he turned off, th' danged horse thief."

Dave scowled, sliding his hand forward to his horse's nose to prevent it from whinnying. He remembered the shifty-eyed individual who'd traded him this horse and got the better of the deal at that. He should have obeyed his warning hunches, but he'd been too anxious to get a fresh horse and keep going. Now he was riding a stolen horse, had been spotted on it, and the sheriff was after him!

If he rode out and tried to explain matters, it would mean hours of delay for a checkup. And another thing—frequently "hoss thieves" got no opportunity to alibi! Dave's throat felt dry and tight as the posse rode slowly back in the deepening darkness peering at the ground.

They missed the spot where he'd turned off. Dave sighed through clenched teeth. He'd wait quietly a few moments and then. . . . Then he saw a deputy wheeling back for another look!

No chance of explanation now after hiding out. Dave drove his spurs home. His startled horse leaped out, hoofs clawing the road. The posse shouted. Dave streaked around a bend in the road. A long straightaway. He spurred desperately for the next curve as guns barked behind him.

The chase went on and on, the quarry neither gaining nor losing as bullets whined past in the straightaways. Sweeping into another straight stretch, Dave, bending low in the saddle, saw a blur of white in the darkness ahead. A roadside marker. The Oregon border. The sheriff's authority would cease beyond that. But sometimes sheriffs ignored little legal points!

Dave spurred and lashed. His horse flattened its ears and streaked ahead. Guns blazed in the night behind him. His horse staggered, then pitched him past the marker. Dave rolled limply until his momentum slowed, then gained his feet and raced into the Oregon brush.

"Too late, men," the sheriff called out. "He's across."

"To heck with the line!" a voice retorted. "We've got him now! Laws ain't made for horse thieves!"

Despite the sheriff's commands a lone horseman rode into the brush. Dave crouched in the shadows. Horseless. Hunted. How would he ever get to Portland in time now, if at all. The rider searched closer, his six-shooter glinting in starlight. As he was about to discover Dave, Dave shoved up on the man's boot with all his strength, toppling him from the saddle. Dave grabbed the saddle horn and swung up as the horse darted ahead in panic. Off in the darkness he reined in and shouted back.

"Sheriff, I'm Dave Remy from the Circle R down in the Sacramento Valley. I didn't steal that dead horse. And I'm just *borrowing* this one. I'll send it back."

He rode into the night. Into Oregon. On his way again to Portland. A long, long way yet. But still on his way.

At Hungry Creek he met a man who was returning to California on a borrowed sorrel. They swapped horses and Dave rode the sorrel to its home corral at Bear Creek. On to Jacksonville for an hour's sleep and a fresh horse. Another night of walking, trotting, galloping. He ate, slept, lived in the saddle on long-legged, easy-gaited horses, chunky pounders, strawberry roans, chestnuts, bays, pintos. Trading a tired horse for a frisky one. Paying some extra cash if he had to. Anything to keep going.

The morning of the fifth day he fell out of the saddle in the little town of Eugene, Oregon. But an hour later he hauled himself onto a new horse. That night he couldn't keep his bloodshot eyes focused. His head bobbed and rolled as though on a swivel. He was too weary to run beside the horse to keep himself awake. Riding at a mad gallop to blow away the cobwebs and pound himself awake, he rode out the horse ahead of schedule.

"How far to Portland?" he murmured, blinking wearily at an innkeeper in French Prairie six mornings after he'd bought the silver spurs.

"Half a day's ride. But you ain't for it, son. Bet your eyes would burn holes in a pillow."

"Not now," Dave snapped. "Get me the fastest horse in town."

He'd have to push and get to the bank before it closed for the day. It wouldn't be open tomorrow if the *Columbia* had arrived in the meantime. Suppose she'd already made port? What would he do then?

At ten thirty that morning he spurred his lathered mount to an auctioneer's corral in Oregon City, his eyes feverishly selecting a horse. At noon he tossed that horse's bridle reins to a boy on the south bank of the Willamette River.

"Ferry to Portland, mister?" another boy called, standing expectantly by a rowboat. Dave shoved it into the river.

"Five dollars if you get me across fast." He squinted toward boats moored on the far side. "The *Columbia* in from Frisco yet?"

"No, sir. Ain't heard the cannon announcin' that she's comin' up the river."

Dave smiled triumphantly and relaxed a bit. The hot sun, the glinting water, the rhythmic creak of the oarlocks made him sleepy, terribly sleepy. He fought to keep his bloodshot eyes open just a little longer. He doused handfuls of water in his face, over his head. *Blam!* The cannon! He forgot sleep.

"Ten dollars more, kid, if. . . ."

He grabbed the gunwhales as the boy stood back mightily on the oars and nearly toppled him overboard. "Golly, fifteen dollars!" the kid grunted. "That's more than Dad makes in a week. He'll think I'm a real man."

Dave stared at his spurs. "Don't get cocky with a pair of silver oars," he muttered. "You might have to make a long hard row with them."

"Huh?"

"Keep rowing," Dave growled, glancing worriedly downriver.

He ran through the streets of Portland, but made himself *walk* into the Adams office, spurs jingling.

"The cashier's out to lunch," a clerk began doubtfully.

"Where?" Dave demanded. A new voice spoke behind him.

"Something I can do for you?"

Dave handed the deposit certificate to a portly gentleman mouthing a gold toothpick.

"Have you any identification?" the man inquired, curiously studying Dave's travel-stained, tousled appearance and bloodshot eyes. He leisurely verified the validity of the certificate, but then suspiciously looked Dave over again.

"Everything seems in order," he said slowly and pointed the toothpick at the certificate. "But there's something odd here. This deposit was made only six days ago down in Sacramento. And the *Columbia* isn't in yet."

"I rode here. Yes, all seven hundred miles," Dave explained, then went on quickly. "I have important business here, but I *missed* catching the *Columbia*. It wouldn't have been safe to carry that amount of gold overland with me."

"Quite true," the man admitted, but still he hesitated.

Dave heard a horse galloping up the street. If he let this pompous bank official stall much longer. . . . "What's wrong with this office?" he snapped. "Haven't you got the gold to. . . ."

"Of course, of course," the man interrupted, smiling reassuringly at eavesdropping customers. The galloping horseman went past the open doors. The official led Dave to a teller.

"Forty pounds of gold. Twelve thousand dollars." The teller smiled. Dave grabbed the bag from the teller and went out into the street just as a shouting mass of men converged on the bank.

"Hello, Jep." Dave smiled wearily at the familiar figure trying to push nearer the front. Jep stared unbelievingly, as Dave handed him the bag of gold. He shook his head slowly.

"How did you do it, kid? Seven hundred miles in six days and nights! You must be made of iron!"

"More like iron that's melting now," Dave said, tottering to stay on his feet. Jep steadied him, then guided him down the street. In a dim room Jep eased him down on a bed, swinging his leaden legs up. He heard Jep's voice from far away.

"Dave, do you want to keep them beautiful spurs on?"

"Uh-uh," Dave murmured, smiling sleepily. "I'm not going to be riding any more nightmares, not for a real long, long while. . . ."

Jep's chuckle faded away as Dave sank luxuriously into the deep velvet blackness of sleep.

Enemy Agent

THOMAS WALSH

He roused slowly, floating up through infinite banks of sleep, in a darkness where he might just as well not have opened his eyes. Before he understood where he was he could feel his heart beating in him like a wire that was being snapped quickly and sharply throughout his body, drawn fast and then snapped again, over and over, at least twice each second. The stillness in the room, beyond the throbbing and completely undisturbed by it, told him nothing; yet he seemed to know a change somewhere. The faintest whisper of sound had wakened him. What was it? He could not remember. It was gone now.

He listened. As he listened he began, unconsciously, to hold his breath. That was a mistake, since a man asleep would not have done so, but he became aware of the fact and of the inference only after his lungs ballooned up solidly inside him. Half erect, with one elbow propping him up, he tried to cover himself by sighing deeply, by grunting an unintelligible word or two, like a man who, after being restless for a moment, was now ready to sleep once more. But at the same time, as soundlessly as possible, he began to slide his hand toward the edge of the bed.

Light stung his eyes, blinding him so that he had to turn his head away from it. He was still on his elbow, but his hand stopped the moment the light hit him. Blinking, starting up as if confused, he muttered something in German.

"Who is there?" a voice repeated after him, but in English. It chuckled dryly. "You understand English," it said. "Oh, yes, Captain Harbecht, Captain Otto Harbecht." It chuckled again. "Stand up now. Not too fast, Captain. And just keep your hands where I can see them."

The man in the bed, heavy eyed, very quiet for a moment or two, pushed a blanket away from him. The flashlight showed him to be fully dressed underneath it, save for shoes, in a German officer's uniform. He was in his late twenties, unshaven and haggard looking; he had black hair, cut close to the skull, and gray eyes that appeared to have been burned into his flesh. After the first instant his face betrayed no expression of any kind.

On his feet, turning away from the flash, he held his arms out from his sides as if he knew quite well what he had to do. A gun touched his back; a hand patted him deftly. Then steps moved away, and a match sputtered into life behind

him. Lantern light, paler and more diffused than that made
by the flash, circled up petulantly across the walls.

"All right," the man with the gun said. "Turn around."

In a room no more than ten feet square, with the bed in
it, one chair, and a bureau wide enough to hold a washbowl
and pitcher, the uniformed man swung himself around
slowly. The other man, who stood near the door, wore a
trench coat and had his gray hat pushed up over his forehead. Young and stocky, very much pleased with himself,
he gestured sideways with the gun in his right hand. "Please
sit down," he said. Despite the note of playful respect in his
voice, he sounded businesslike, crisp, quite sure of himself.
"Your shoes are there, Captain, by the bed. Put them on."
He was obeyed passively. Nothing of the uniformed man's
anger, of his weary disgust with himself, was apparent. He
had meant to rest only for an hour or two, not to sleep. And
then the moment he pulled the blanket over him. . . .

He began to lace his shoes, but without hurrying. "I suppose it's still raining," he said. He spoke like an Englishman,
precisely, rather sharply. The man with the gun, relaxed if
vigilant in the doorway, tapped it against his right leg.

"You gave us a lot of trouble," he said. "But when you
jumped off the train Tuesday, it didn't take us long to find
out just about where that happened. You were seen here
and there too. You were seen this afternoon in the boat you
found. At first we thought you got over the river in it; then
I decided that the fog might have fooled you. Do you know
what you're on? An island, Captain Harbecht—a big island,
but an island just the same. You couldn't see much of it in
the fog, and when you landed you thought you were safely
across, eh?"

He smiled, lowered his jaw, scratched it with the gun, and shrugged. "But you weren't. Not quite, Captain Harbecht." He pronounced the name slowly, relishing it. "When we couldn't find any trace of you, two of us came out here to look things over. Not very hopefully. But in bed, asleep— that was stupid, wasn't it, Captain?"

"Yes," the uniformed man said. "*Stupid* is the word."

From the side of the bed, bent forward slightly, he drew one of the shoelaces into a bow. After that, briefly, his right hand was hidden between his feet. His revolver was under the bed, four or five inches back; all the time he had been afraid the stocky man would catch a glitter of light on it. His fingers closed on it and whipped it up between his knees.

There was no time to say what he had intended to say: "Drop your gun." The man near the door jumped back, his face savage suddenly, and fired before he had his gun all the way down. The uniformed man, who understood what choice he had then, shot simultaneously.

"Blasted fool," he said low, to himself. His voice was uneven. He wiped the sleeve of the uniform across his forehead, got up, and went over to the doorway. They would search him, of course, he had known that, but there seemed to be no good reason why they should search the room. When he lay down at dusk, even though he had not intended to sleep, he had listened to a half-understood need for caution. The Americans would have called it an ace in the hole, he remembered. Well, he had needed it.

In the doorway he dropped to one knee, and then rose immediately. Two of them, he thought; the one with him must be around somewhere. He snuffed out the lantern, crossed the dark outer room to the door, and listened there. Fog drifted by in wisps and streamers; ten feet away it clustered around the nearest tree and blurred it shapelessly. But no one called out. No one came running. A big island, he thought, with the other off somewhere, far enough so that he had not heard the shots. When he was sure of that he groped back carefully to the bedroom.

The flash gave him all the light he needed there, a narrow strip centered blindly against the far wall of the room. In it his movements were half-seen, half-shadowy gestures as he stripped off the uniform and got into a brown suit, a trench coat, a gray felt hat. He had to have them; he felt no revulsion in taking them. Once they found the other man—even before perhaps—they would not worry too much about taking him alive. Not Captain Otto Harbecht.

He knew that, and he acted on it. Only a fool would have thrown away his chance.

In one of the coat pockets there was a wallet; in another, cigarettes; in a third a draft card made out to Albert Joseph Bender, of Brooklyn, New York. The dark man looked at that and then at Bender with a certain impassive regard in his eyes. But he could not resist the cigarettes. He even delayed long enough to smoke one in hungry draughts, hiding it in his palm whenever he looked out through the open door. After it began to scorch his lips he pulled up the trench coat around his throat, snapped the cigarette through the doorway, and followed it.

Outside, it was damp rather than cold, the fog misty white, packed down solidly over the ground. The cabin faded, vanishing before he was halfway to the river. Five minutes or so later he found the boat behind a fringe of bushes where he had hidden it that afternoon, but he had a bad few moments

71-3381   Napoleon Public Library

until one of his knees banged painfully into the hard wood. He pushed it out to the water, knelt in it, and shoved himself clear with a thrust of his free leg. At once he was gliding through a white world distorted by occasional raw puffs of air.

He began to row, trying to keep parallel with the shore, not near enough to be seen from it, yet not too far out to lose it entirely. It was the only guide he had. When he reached the end and swung right, he knew he would be headed for the far side of the river.

A dock behind him, very low in the water, stopped him with a horribly loud smash and a shock that almost toppled him backward. At the same moment something far off, a plane or a boat, began to roll ugly coughs of sound at him through the fog.

A boat, he decided presently. But he could wait where he was and be safe, too. Tonight they could pass twenty yards away and never see him. It was odd, though, that almost at once the sound seemed to beat at him from every direction, getting louder and closer second by second. That was just the fog, he told himself, twisting it, making it seem to be right on top of him. He waited, the revolver dug in between his thighs, one corner of his mouth twitching a little. They wouldn't find him in this fog. Couldn't, he thought. What was he jumpy for?

An orange glow, blurred at first as if set behind innumerable folds of white gauze, appeared on the left. He cursed suddenly, furiously; the dock, of course, that was what they were trying to find, and he had never suspected.

Two strokes brought him back against it, the only way to go then, because they were between him and the river, and edging in slowly. The glow strengthened. It glared sullenly on him, like a circle of frosted glass that had caught and compressed in itself all the quality of light in the fog, as he jumped off to the dock. It went by, stopped, groped for him, passed him, swung back. Somebody shouted.

He bent low, running for the island. Three or four lashes of sound spattered after him viciously. The last one was close.

He ran faster then, shoving himself aside from a tree that sprang suddenly out of the mist by thrusting his arms against it. No panic, he was telling himself. That would be foolish. That would be playing into their hands. Yet he ran on until his thighs got numb under him. Afterward, too, he managed to struggle ahead one way or another.

Finally he sank down, sobbing for breath, when a bit of earth crumbled under him and threw him sideways. For a long time he lay still at the foot of the slope, with a rock as big as a dining-room table looming over him. As soon as he could move, he crawled over to it and crouched down in back of it. It was a big island. In the fog, he thought, they could never find him. Not till morning. If he was quiet now, if he did not make a sound, he would be all right. Yes. He was conscious, not of fear but of an intolerable sensation of watchfulness and strain. Each time they shouted at one another or made a noise in the underbrush, he would wait rigidly, one arm on the rock ready to pull him erect, the other hand holding the revolver shoulder high.

After a while they must have realized that if he heard them he could tell where they were. It became still then, and the stillness was more difficult to endure than the sounds had been. He felt that he wanted them to come, he actually thought of shouting at them; but that passed, by the time he could breathe normally again, and was replaced by a desperate craving to know the hour. Ten o'clock? Midnight? Two in the morning? He had no idea. In an attempt to limit it in some way he tried to build up a sequence of events in his head.

At dusk, when he landed on the island, when he thought he was safely across the river, it must have been five thirty or six. Then he saw the bungalow and went in because there might have been a can of food inside. It was fifty-odd hours since he had eaten or slept. He found no food, but he lay down for a little while. Not to sleep, no. Just to rest till it got dark. After that, time withdrew into a secret place of its own, where he could not find it and measure it. How long had he slept when Bender found him? Two hours? Three? Four?

There was no way to judge. What was clear was that he would probably be safe here till dawn, but only till dawn. By daylight, with enough men to beat from one side of the island to the other, they'd find him. Yet if he knew the time now, how many hours of darkness there were left him, he might be able to think of some way to get clear of the island. Had he one hour to work with—four, five?

The oddest impression of darkness flowing away, rushing away, touched him and spread out a little, sending tingling urges through his body. Could he close his eyes, empty his mind of everything, and feel the time it was? He tried that, and it was absurd, of course. In the end his thoughts came back to the thing they had never really left—a boat.

There were three of those: the one he had found, the one Bender and the other man had landed in, and the motorboat.

They would be guarded. He could swim. . . . He stopped
there. Of itself, instantly, the word brought up a mental
and physical depression that warned him against it. Not that
way, he thought; if he covered fifty yards he'd be pushing his
luck. The other side of the river might be that close, but
probably it was not. So he had to get a boat—had to, had
to, had to.

He stood up while that phrase repeated itself senselessly
in his mind. It would have been foolish to risk a cigarette,
but he put one between his lips, sucking the dry end, and it
was more help than he had thought it would be. There was
only one place where he could find a boat—at the dock. But
if he went back there. . . . He began to consider it, letting
his thoughts move a step at a time. They would have guards
there, but probably not so many as on the far side of the
island, where he should have headed for, logically. Perhaps
there would be only one guard. One, he thought.

It seemed fantastic at first, and then it wasn't fantastic
at all. Risk it, he thought. Why not? There was no other way
at all.

Even though he decided that firmly inside himself, minute
passed after minute before he could force himself away from
the rock, which seemed then to be a place he had known,
and been safe in, all his life. Once he began to move, it was
not so bad, because the fog, the lovely fog, more beautiful
and more comforting than anything he could remember,
hung thickly before his eyes. He would move half a dozen
steps through it, and listen, and go on once more, and listen
once more. Now and again he had to stop, fighting a panic
that tried to hurry him on recklessly, waiting until he could
press it down, small and fluttery, inside him. And later, be-

fore he could have been halfway back to the dock, shouts
rose up and clamored in the woods behind him.

They had heard something there, an animal, he thought.
Did they know it was an animal? He pictured them gathered
somewhere, beating together in a circle, the boats forgotten.
With that thought in him, he could not help himself. He had
to move faster, his heart racing, the slightest sound, each
puff of wind, shocking him rigid.

Suddenly the river was before him, a black sheet rolling
away in the fog. He skirted it carefully, almost imperceptibly.
Minutes later—hours to him—he saw a lantern hung breast
high at the end of the dock. Beyond it, no more than twenty
feet away, he saw a boat.

It was the boat he had used before. The fools, he thought—
everything shaking inside him—the incredible fools. Off there
chasing a rabbit, leaving the boat here for anyone. . . . No,
he thought then, coldly, savagely. He was the fool to think it
would be as simple as that. They knew he'd look for a boat,
that he had to find one; it was here, but there was someone
with it, a watcher. Someone who would wait out there on the
dock, perhaps in the trees, until he came. All the details were
arranged: the lamp, the boat, the man waiting for him. A
good shot—this time they meant to take no chances—the
man would be someone who understood perfectly what he
had to do.

"Wait," they probably told him, "wait here for him. He'll
see the boat, and he might listen for a minute or two, till he's
sure there's no one around. Then he'll run for it. Don't call
to him. Just use your gun, and make sure you don't miss. It's
simple enough that way. He's dangerous, and he got Bender,
didn't he? Well, then."

All that was clear, and yet, despite it, there was a tiny spark of hope left somewhere in him. If he had not been heard, if the guard had no idea he was so close now, there was still some kind of chance for him. The guard would not be quiet forever; he'd move, shift his body, perhaps light a cigarette for a puff or two. Then, he thought, I'll have him; then I'll know where he is and how to handle him. So, if I'm careful now; if I'm patient. . . .

Time passed, endless time. Water lapped and murmured against the dock, and the noise in the woods, farther off, barely came to him. By then his mind was working erratically, in brief starts, abrupt stops. Suppose there is no watcher? Suppose I am a fool to wait here? They'll be back soon, and then it will be too late. But now, with a bit of courage, why now, man, it's right out there waiting for you.

He took a few unsteady and shallow breaths, like a man bracing himself against physical torture. Every time he looked out at the boat he felt himself turning fiercely hot and reckless, as if nothing, not one guard or ten, could stop him from reaching the boat, once he ran for it.

There was one tree, the last one, between him and the dock. He moved over to it silently and rested against it, but even from there he saw no one, he heard nothing.

Now, he thought. Or was he going to stay here until they came back and found him? His jaws were clenched together until the bones ached. Should he wait five minutes more? Count three hundred, say, slowly? Then he'd know. Then he'd be sure. One . . . two. . . . At first he was able to make himself pause like that between the numbers, but soon they began to crowd over one another in his head.

It must be getting lighter, too; a new kind of grayness,

not altogether of the fog, thinned and wavered over him. He looked up at it with bloodshot eyes. Fourteen, he thought. Fifteen . . . sixteen . . . seventeen . . . eighteen-nineteen-twenty. . . .

He heard someone grunt. He heard underbrush crackle under a body shifting to a more comfortable position. Not far away, just on the other side of the rock. The recklessness left him; he felt as patient as time, and as remorseless. When the crackle died, after rasping across his eardrums like hard chalk, he slid himself away from the tree. Moving his feet ahead by inches, shifting his weight in turn from one to the other without lifting them from the thin grass, he found himself helped occasionally by the other man's bored restlessness. A deep breath up there, a peevish yawn. His right foot eased into a stone. He picked it up and held it. In fifteen minutes he covered perhaps fifteen feet.

A tree, quite thick enough to hide a man, pushed through the fog at him. Someone got up fretfully on the other side of it, and he froze where he was. His breathing stopped. There was no doubt about what the grayness was now. Black, naked branches took shape in it; a path ran back under his feet.

He raised his gun. He tossed the stone in his left hand down the path. It thumped there, bounced. A shadow moved around the tree in front of him, rifle up almost to its shoulder. Instantly, and much faster than he had ever thought he could move, he smashed his gun three times into the side of its head.

After that he saw everything—boat, lamp, dock, water—through wavering reddish streaks. Even then he never expected to reach the boat alive. Wouldn't there be another guard waiting for him? Yet he did not hurry. With the gun in his hand he almost strolled out to the dock, looked around him there, then bent and cast off the rope. There were no shots, no sounds anywhere. A moment after he got into the boat the fog swept over him and the island vanished.

Done, he thought. Now. He began to row. His cheeks, puffed up hotly under his eyes, bothered him. A curious and empty ringing, an echo of silence, circled out and out through his head. When he had rowed for some distance, he dug his right oar into the water and pulled hard on the left one. Apparently he was clear of the island; he passed the place where it should have been, and another fifty feet, without seeing a sign of it.

He was all right then. Straight in back of him, minutes away, was the far side of the river. He rested awhile. The stillness about him, the remote pure secrecy of a white world hushed and empty, seemed to be all he wanted. He saw it, felt it, heard it, smelled it, almost tasted it. Back there on the dock he had walked out toward death without caring very much whether it came or not, but now everything was changed. Now, in his flesh, in his mind, too, he felt nakedly and passionately and thankfully alive.

Dawn, he thought. The fog streamed up in odd bulges, uneasily; through it he could see stretches of clear gray water, another world revealing itself bit by bit in narrow aisles, in pools of limpid and sunless serenity. Far behind him the motorboat churned into life.

They've discovered the guard, he thought. They know where I'm headed for. He began to row again, not far this time. Before they had rounded the island he stepped out of the boat and edged it back into the current. Let them find

him now. He looked out at the boat and saluted briskly, but
with some derision. Good luck, he thought; the best of everything from Herr Kapitän Otto Harbecht.

On a strip of beach, with a short but sharp upward rise
behind it to some trees that almost overhung the river, he
took off the trench coat and threw it into a clump of reeds.
If they knew about Bender they knew about the coat. Get
rid of it then, so that they couldn't spot him at once by it.
He turned, vigorous, resolute, almost cheerful, to the bank
that was no more than a foot or two over his head. There
were roots up there, digging down through the earth; his
hands were on them, ready to pull him up, when he heard
two men moving toward him through the woods.

They stopped just over him. There was no place to hide,
no time either. All he could do was to press himself flat
against the bank, his head twisted up painfully.

They would go by, he thought. They could not know he
was there, or they would have been much more careful. So,
in a moment. . . .

He thought of the rowboat and looked around at it. It
bobbed gently offshore, thick curls of fog twining up over it
without altogether obscuring it. The bow swung away from
him, then swung round again in a lazy circle. Thirty seconds
more, ten feet or so farther out into the river, and they would
not be able to see it from the shore. Half a minute, he
thought, his gray eyes luminous as a child's. All that he had
endured—hunger, exhaustion, the island, the night, Bender—
he would have endured again to have that time pass instantly,
in a breath.

But it happened that only part of it went by, ten, perhaps
twelve seconds. Then one voice broke off into a startled ex-

clamation over him, and the other cursed huskily. A branch
snapped as though it had been thrust aside—to see better, he
thought. Now that they knew where the boat was they'd
jump down to the beach. They'd find him there. It was over.

He did not feel sorry. He felt relieved, if he felt anything.
That was shameful, and he knew it was shameful, and yet
he could not help it. In the end it might come down to the
fact that a man could stand so much, and then he was done.
He turned. At least it would be quicker this way, he thought.
No questions. A few shots. Well, he'd tried. That was all
anyone could do.

Then the motorboat, very close now, droned up louder
through the mass of fog brooding low over the water. One of
the men on the bank shouted at it, then fired twice, apparently into the air. The next moment it sliced out of the fog
as if it had been waiting for those things. The two over him
roared together, excitedly. "That way!" they cried. He could
picture the way their arms were thrust out. "That way,
quick!"

They saw him from the boat—that was the part he could
not understand at first—but they did not stop or fire at him.
They just swung in close to shore, while one of the figures by
the rail lifted an arm at him. Then the slim black shape vanished again, and the men on the bank began to crash away
after it.

He stood there as if he could not move. They had seen
him. Why hadn't they. . . .

Then he knew the reason for that *why*. From the motorboat they must have been three men standing close together
in a group. Two were on the bank, one just under them on
the beach. It seemed incredible—it was, indeed, a source after-

ward of many long and bitter arguments—that the two above had never seen the one below them.

His eyes closed for a moment or two. A bit of luck, he thought. Well, maybe he had it coming to him. He reached up and took hold of the roots again and climbed the bank. That night, three or four hours after dark, he crossed the Swiss border.

Two men talked about him next morning in a private office at Gestapo headquarters in Berlin.

"Higginson," one of them said. He was a small man with thin brown hair and coolly venomous brown eyes. "James Percival Higginson. . . . It's a little late now to tell me who he is, I think."

The other man mopped his forehead with his handkerchief. He said, "Everything was done that could be done. I hope you understand that. He passed himself off as a certain Captain Otto Harbecht, home on leave from the Russian front. I don't know how he got into Germany, or what he wanted. But. . . ."

"But we know how he got out," the first man said. "We know that, don't we?" He looked across the desk placidly enough, but for some reason the other man found it necessary to use his handkerchief again. "As to what he wanted— if they are thinking of an invasion, they will require very precise information as to the number of planes we produce these days. This Higginson, as Captain Otto Harbecht, probably got that information. He got away from you, and he killed Bender. There are men not so valuable to us as Bender was. He spoke English like one of those Yankees; he was even registered in their draft. When we got him back to

America, after the training we gave him here, he could have been very useful to us. You agree, Stromer?"

Stromer agreed. Yes. Of course. But that Englishman— they had him cornered on the Berlin Express. When he opened a window and jumped out, it was going so fast that he should have been killed. But he got away, and he got away from them on the island, too. Sometimes they had the devil's own luck.

"And sometimes," the first man said, "they are helped by stupidity. But we shall attend to that, Stromer. At once."

Stromer looked into his handkerchief. There was no need for him to say anything.

Of course, James Percival Higginson did not call it the devil's own luck. He never talked very much about it. When he showed up in London sometime later, he said it had been a bit of a run, but not bad, considering. Once he reached Switzerland there had been nothing to it at all.

The Iron Lady

CONRAD RICHTER

The old man in the big house heard the carriage stop and the sound of men's voices. He guessed what they wanted. Let them come, he said to himself, and his lip twitched in sardonic humor. Others had come before them, and none had got the secret out of him yet. But they'd better move fast. Wasn't he supposed to be on his deathbed? Any day now his mind might not be clear or he might be gone to that bourn from which no man returneth, or so the parson on his visits to cheer the sick had told him.

Well, it was true he was old and had taken to his bed. But he wasn't laid out yet, not by a long shot. He wasn't even

48

upstairs. He'd ordered his housekeeper, the cook, and the yard man to fetch his bed down. He told them it would save them running upstairs with trays and downstairs with slops, but all the time he and they knew the real reason. He didn't want to give up being among the living. He didn't want to leave this corner room on the first floor he called his office. Most of his life had been spent here with his high desk and stool, his low desk table and chair with the familiar worn red cushion. Here were his shelves of furnace accounts and records, on the wall a row of wooden pegs with his clothes, including his blue army overcoat, his cocked hat and sword.

Upstairs, the green clutter of leaves shut out everything. Down here he could look out and see his furnace against the hill, built of the same gray-brown stone as the house, everything still intact outside and in, even the ore barrows and charcoal wagons on the upper level. The stack needed only ore, limestone, and charcoal to be fired. But the brown-painted shutters on the furnace were closed tight and the experienced eye saw no heat waves rising against the sky.

He could hear the men now entering the iron gate to the grounds. They would lower their voices presently. The house always sobered people when they got close—the huge, solid bulk of it, the tiers of white shutters against the mountain stone, the large windows with their small panes, the big front door with the carved window light above, and the long lights on either hand. The furnace men used to say that if the sidelights would swing with the door, you could drive a team through.

The bell on its long rope tinkled. Presently the old man could hear Manda moving through the house to answer it. His lips pursed in ironic anticipation. They were curious lips seen sometimes on the Scotch; not exactly thick, but ropy, as if they got in the way, and he had them always to contend with. Ansell Sloan had white hair above, while a ring of the same ran below from his ears like a thin strip of hairy hide pasted around his bare chin. In this frame his face looked like that of a crabbed but lovable saint, so that you forgot the uncompromising lips and wondered how a man with such a gentle, wry face could have had the nickname of Iron Sloan as a soldier before he became an ironmaster.

You could see the strangers relax when they saw him. The house and grounds might be formidable, but this old man would be easy to handle. He didn't look like an iron soldier to them. They were shrewd, sharp-eyed men from Union-town, with fine clothes and well-fed faces. First they com-plimented him on the house and grounds. Then they asked about the two paintings.

"This one toward the road was my wife," he said. "The other one, with the flowers under it, was my mother-in-law."

"Isn't that a little unusual, General?" one of them asked, smiling. "Flowers for your mother-in-law?"

"Not for Mary Harris," the old man said, quickly. "But that's a long story."

They didn't press him. They were interested in something else, something more valuable than a mother-in-law.

"We understand, General, that not all your iron came from the Cornwall mines." The leader of the group got down to business. "You told some people, I believe, that the best quality iron you ever had came from a secret source of your own."

"Ah!" The ironmaster rubbed a stubbly chin. "So you heard this even as far as Uniontown?"

"It's true then, General, that you owed your success to a secret iron mine?"

"Well, yes, I guess it's true, though I wouldn't call it an iron mine. It's just where my best iron came from. But remember now I didn't say where I got it."

The men licked their lips and hitched closer. "Was this source pretty far away? Did it cost you much to freight it here?"

"Didn't cost me hardly nothing."

"You say it was very rich iron?"

"About the best I ever knew."

"Was it worked out?"

"God bless you, no. It gave iron to some others who knew about it, and still does to me when I need it."

You could see victory now on their faces. "Will you, for a consideration, General, draw us a map of the location?"

"No, I couldn't do that."

There was consternation on their faces. "Why not?"

"Because I don't think you could find it."

"That would be our risk. This iron is still in existence?"

"Well, yes, some of it. But the source has moved."

"Moved? How could it move? You said it was never worked out."

"That's true," he agreed.

He could see with enjoyment that they were completely baffled, that they thought him a queer old man. Well, maybe he was. You got queer sometimes in your eighties. Not that they gave up easily. For more than an hour they pestered and cross-examined him. In the end, like the others, they had to go without it, saying they would be back again.

He sat chuckling dryly when they had left. So they wanted

to buy his iron mine? Well, they weren't the first, and likely wouldn't be the last. But never would he tell them. They wouldn't believe it had been a woman. They wouldn't understand what he was talking about. You had to live back in the 1750's to understand. Today, in the Millburn Valley, you saw mostly fields of grain and corn, with plenty of cattle, grass, fat barns, and peaceful farmhouses. But then all was solid woods and swamps with thick vines running up the big butts in the bottoms, with cabins buried in the wild greenness, with alarms from the savages twice a year and waking up some morning to find your neighbors killed and their cabins burned. You might even wake up and find it done to your own folks.

That's what had happened to him, and him only eight years old. When he fought back and cried, one of the savages gave him a blow, and he remembered nothing till they shook him and threw water on him to get him going. For a week after that, it seemed, they dragged him through the forest, first a large party, then just two, tying him to one or the other of them, jerking him through bogs and runs, driving him over logs and roots. Hardly was he alive when they reached the other Indian party, waiting for them with a captive at a hemlock spring.

Never as long as he lived would he forget the sight of this unknown spot in the wilderness, with the black mountain above, the painted savage faces around the fire below, the ghastly flutter of scalps on stretchers, and sitting on the ground nearby the young white captive, Mary Harris, with her baby at her breast. She wore a gray homespun short gown, muddied and torn by the bush. Her hair was black,

her face brown. She was barefoot and her legs badly scratched
by roots and briers. Her state looked hopeless, and yet the way
she sat there, living for herself, paying no attention to her
captors or her fate, gave him the first sensation of life and
hope since he was taken. He tried to run to her, but the
Indian he was tied to jerked him and he fell to the ground.

He got to his feet, shaken and trembling. Had she sympa-
thized with him a lick by word or look, his tears would have
turned into a flood.

"Don't mind them; they don't know no better," she said
matter-of-factly.

"They killed my ma and pa!" he cried.

She made resigned noises with her tongue, like a grandmother. "Maybe your ma and pa are lucky. They don't need
to go through what me and you do."

"I wish they'd a killed me too."

"Oh, no, you don't," she said dully, almost flatly. "They
broke in a young boy's head for cryin' a ways back. You
don't wish you was him a-lyin' back there with his brains on
a tree."

What she said sickened him. He pitied himself. To show
how bad he felt, he made himself cry noisily. To his surprise,
she turned her head away. He bawled and cried, but she acted
as if she didn't know he was there. He called out the most
pitiful things to make her feel sorry for him, so he could cry
with more reason, but she might have been stone-deaf for all
the notice of it she took. He found his eyes drying up despite
himself. Though he tried to fetch tears again, none would
come. Bitterness and hate for her rose in him instead.

"Don't you know me? I'm Ansell Sloan! They call me
Andy in Black Run!" he cried at her.

He might as well have been crying to the wind. She sat calm and contained, attending her baby. That puny thing and herself were all that mattered to her. She was like an Indian herself, and next day when they moved through the woods, he watched her carry her pack of savage booty like a squaw. Not once did he hear her rebel or complain. He was only a boy, but twice with spirit he threw off the stolen horns heavy with powder they had hung around his neck. In the end, he had to carry them anyhow, along with the cuts and bruises they gave him.

Now wouldn't you reckon she'd feel for him when his captors beat him so that he would sob for a long time afterward? But hardly a word from her, except to taunt him for bawling. Then hate for her would make him stop quick enough. No sooner would they camp in the evening and the fire at dusk set him crying for home than she would mock him for it until he answered in kind.

The Indians only laughed and egged them on. This was a big joke to them, something that gave the savages pleasure—two white persons who couldn't stand together against their common enemy, but fought each other. Most always after a fight between them, the Indians treated her better and slackened her bonds.

"Injun pet! Turncoat!" He scorned her more than once, but she gave him no notice that she had heard.

For days the party marched through the woods. Once they stopped while two of their men stole away to bring back mysterious news in their own language. Next morning the party split, and the captives were left in camp under the guard of a savage they called Onchedunk. Andy cried when the Indian tied him so tight that it hurt.

"Watch out. Don't cross him," Mary Harris warned. "He's the one that massacreed the other boy."

"You care more about that other boy than me!" Andy accused.

"I ought to," Mary Harris said bitterly. "He was my own Billy."

Andy looked at her with a sudden start. He was sober now. His eyes went dry. He stared uneasily at the savage who had done it, his face painted in colors that had run in the rain so that they distorted his features. A large bunch of hair from some former scalping had been dyed bright red and fixed to the top of his head, while a piece of bright metal hung from his nose and covered much of his mouth, so that he looked like a picture of the devil.

Now how could Mary Harris let such a terrifying creature hurt her and never a whimper? He trussed her so that hardly could she hold her babe. He pulled on the knots so it must have cut into her woman's flesh. And all the time he was the one who had killed and scalped her own boy before her eyes. And yet her face hardly changed. Not a complaint did she make. Then Onchedunk took his gun and left.

It wasn't long afterward when a flock of migrating birds mostly with red-speckled breasts, swarmed into camp, picking up crumbs from around the fire. They must have taken the two bound prisoners for stumps, for they flittered close to both, and especially the young woman, chittering and chirping until finally they flew off into the woods.

"Them birds say anything to you?" Mary Harris asked, when they had gone.

"Birds can't talk," the boy told her.

"Oh, they don't talk sniveling and pigeonhearted like you,"

she said. "Their talk was spunky and cheerful. They said,
What was I doin' here? Why didn't I up and go?"

The boy looked at Mary Harris strangely. He had heard
that being captured by Indians sometimes affected white
minds. Now he saw her begin to inch herself and child
toward the fire. When she got there, she struggled to hold
her bound bare legs over the low flame. The boy watched.
He saw the white ankles grow black with burn, but still she
kept them there. Several times her legs tried to burst the
bonds, but she had to put herself again to the fire. In the
end, the rawhide snapped, but not until a long, painful time
had passed. Then she moved quickly to the pile of booty.
With her bare toes she pulled out a rusty ax taken from some
ravaged white cabin. Holding the blade up between her feet,
she bent forward and severed the thongs binding her arms.

Now wasn't it a shame that this was when Onchedunk
chose to return. They heard him coming. She tried to
get back where she had been, putting the broken strips of
hide around her, but before she was settled, he was there.
Never in his life would the boy forget the look on the returned Indian's face—a look of fierce rage that she had tried
to escape. With the barrel of his gun, he gave her a blow
that knocked her over on the ground.

The baby screamed.

"Give um!" Onchedunk said, dropping his gun and holding out his hands for the child.

When she refused, he tore at the baby with both hands.
Then she let it go sooner than see its tiny arms pulled from
their sockets. Twisting his face, Onchedunk lifted it up to
dash the small head against a tree. At the sight, Mary Harris
sprang like a she-panther. She snatched up the rusty ax and

went for him. The Indian saw her coming and quickly laid down the screaming child, motioning for her to do the same with the ax.

"No, you wily snake in the grass!" she answered, and the boy had never seen her eyes so black. "You'd murder us both!"

It was doubtful if the savage understood the words, but he did her face and manner. Jerking at the hatchet in his belt with one hand, he reached for his gun with the other. Before he got hold of it, she was on him with her weapon.

"Now it's either you or us!" she cried.

The boy shut his eyes. He heard a confused series of sounds, but except for the screaming of the baby, he couldn't tell what they were. In his heart he believed that no half-starved, barefooted white woman, not even an outraged mother, could be a match for this Indian. The crying of the baby suddenly ceased. He shuddered, closing his eyes the tighter, waiting for his own end.

"You can look now. It's all over," he heard Mary Harris say. When he opened his eyes, the Indian lay on his face, and the baby was back in the arms of its mother.

"Did you kill him?" he stammered.

"He'd a took our hair, but we won't take his," she said.

"He looks so—bloody," Andy whimpered.

"How do you expect him to look?" she demanded. "You want your enemies done away with before they do away with you, but you want somebody else to do it someplace where you can't see it. Well, sometimes God Almighty puts you in a place where you got to do it your own self as best you can."

It took only a few moments to cut his thongs.

"I don't know whether to leave you or take you along," she said. "They'll likely kill you if they catch us. But they'll kill you for spite if they find you still here."

She scratched the booty pile, hunting for food. There was nothing save a doeskin bag of spoiled meal, crawling with worms, and a small piece of dried venison, dark and rock hard. Andy tried to take a captured musket. He lifted its terrible weight.

"It's not for the puny," Mary Harris said. Barefooted, with only the hunk of venison and her child, she started off, taking to the woods instead of the path by which they had come.

"That's not the way," the boy protested.

"They won't look for us so quick in the brush," she said.

Once away from camp, freedom was almost too sweet to bear. They had escaped from the savages at last. Every wild glade looked good. A tiny stream ran across their way, and they lay down on its mossy bank to drink. Before they were on their feet they heard a savage hallooing far in the leafy reaches behind them.

"They come back and found him," Mary said grimly.

Soon the sound of a musket echoed among the hills. A little later, faintly and from a great distance, came an answer, not one shot, but two. After an interval the nearer rifle sounded again. This time Mary Harris didn't speak. Both of them knew what it meant. Whoever had returned had sounded the alarm. His distant companions had heard and answered, telling him they were on the way back and, whatever the trouble, would soon be there to help.

The boy hurried on as best he could. He was still free, but only now did he recognize what a terrible freedom it was, a hundred and fifty miles or more in the wilderness, with no roads, just Indian paths and streams that ran as freely in Indian country as in white, and with signs that could be read only by the savages who had the country mapped out in their minds.

They kept going that day until they could no longer see. That night no painful thongs dug into the boy's flesh, but neither was there the comfort of a fire. He lay close to Mary Harris for warmth and for protection against the black unknown. Not for a minute would he have admitted it to her. He had long since learned not to try to enlist her pity. But just being with her made him feel stronger, and the closer the stronger.

At the first glimmer of light through the trees, they were off, stumbling through the fog-choked woods. As a captive he had had little concern about missing the way. Now their lostness and vast uncertainty in the woods lay on him. But if Mary Harris felt anything, she didn't show it.

"We got sunup to foller in the morning and sunset to keep at our back in the evening. What more do you want?" she said.

Oh, she was a hard taskmaster and let him take no easy way. Once they broke out of the woods into a wild open meadow of coarse grass. It was like coming alive again for the boy, but she plunged him quick as she could into a dense forest of hemlock and pine, where it was dark even by day and the ground lay carpeted with brown needles.

"They won't track us so easy in here," she said.

More than once they came on trails in the forest, not the narrow deer paths that soon petered out. These were wider trails, plainly made by human feet. They looked inviting, a far easier road than over logs and through the brush. The boy would have gladly taken one of them, but Mary Harris would have none of one or the other.

"That's where they'd lay to jump us," she said.

It was late afternoon when they came out on the bushy, bald knob of a hill. This, they could see, was the end of the forest valley they had been traveling since they left camp. Ahead lay two valleys. They couldn't see much, just the wooded openings to each. Now which should they take? Both seemed to lead in an easterly direction. Later they were to learn that only one ran east. The other gradually turned and led south and back to the western wilderness and the Indians.

For a long time they stood ragged and puzzled, trying to think. Even Mary Harris seemed unable to decide. As they waited, a twittering of birds grew closer in the trees and a flock of red-speckled breasts landed in the bushes about them.

"Why, them look like those same birds that came to our camp," Mary Harris said.

As they watched, the flock, with sudden unity, took wing and flew down the left of the unknown valleys. The boy saw a look of cruel resolve come over his companion's face.

"I listened to them before, and I'll listen to them again," she said, and started to follow.

It turned out to be a rough, discouraging valley, filled with obstructions that boded no good for their choice. The second afternoon the boy said he could make it no farther, not till tomorrow anyway. He was plumb worn out. He lay on his face on a drift of last year's leaves. No, he wouldn't get up anymore today. Mary Harris had to lay down her child to yank him to his feet. The moment the baby was set on the ground, it started to squall. The squalling must have sounded a long way through the woods. Far off, they heard an Indian halloo, then an answer from the mountain.

At the terrible sound, the boy got to his feet quickly enough. He trembled so much that Mary Harris had to lead him to a fallen hemlock tree. They climbed its prostrate trunk until hidden in its thickest branches. Settled here for only a little while, they heard the unmistakable click of a ramrod in a rifle barrel. Then all was silent, but they knew that an Indian stood nearby, listening for the first sound to give them away.

More than once Andy had complained on the journey that he didn't care if he lived or died, if the savages got him or not. But now that one actually stood only yards away, it terrified him. Every minute he feared the baby would cry again. The smallest sound or gurgle must betray their hiding place. Hour after hour, Mary Harris sat stolidly with the child pressed tightly against her breast. It slept on, and when it awoke she nursed it. What nourishment it could find in its mother's starved body, the boy didn't know. Never had day held on so long. The savage must have gone, he thought. But when dusk fell thick on the woods, they knew he had been there all the time. Still only rods away, he uttered a terrible yell. Then they heard him leave, hallooing to his distant companion.

Before leaving the fallen tree in the morning, they had the last of the carefully treasured hunk of venison. Black, hard, and tasteless as it was, Andy hated to see it go. Now nothing stood between them and starvation. That day they splashed through a swamp where the trees stood gaunt and lifeless above them and the brown stagnant water smelled of death.

They chewed the tendrils of the wild grapevines for food
and ate what tiny applelike fruits of the wild thorn trees
they could find. Of all the country they went through, the
thorn-tree thickets were the worst, whipping them, tearing
their clothing to shreds, leaving long, bloody scratches on
their bodies.

Wherever darkness overtook them, they spent the night,
once in a region of rocks, once in a brake of rhododendrons.
Hope each morning was soon succeeded by daze and exhaustion. What day of the week or month it was, neither of them
had any notion. The morning after the thorn-thicket passage,
the boy fell down and couldn't get up.

"You go on," he told her. "Let the Injuns get me."

"You always got to fight something in this life," she said.
"If it ain't Injuns, it's something else."

"I can't fight no more," he told her.

She had to take a stick then to beat him up, like the
savages did, and after that she wouldn't let him sit down.

"You're worse'n the Injuns!" he cried at her.

"Go holler and bring 'em on. You'll find out who's the
worser," she told him.

"You're a devil!" he sobbed at her another time.

"You ain't seen half of me yet," she promised. "Lay down
again and you'll find out."

He called her all the mean names he had ever heard. Had
he known she was like this, never would he have left camp
with her. But nothing he said did any good. She kept driving
him on. Just the same, he could tell she was weakening. Her
gray dress, long whipped by the brush, hung on her in rags.
Her arms and legs and face were bleeding. Next morning,
through half-closed eyes, he watched her. After nursing her

young one, hardly could she draw herself up by a sapling to her feet.

She can't go far any more, he kept telling himself that day. Then we can both lay down and die together.

Around noon he thought she was ready to give up. She had turned on him a glazed eye. "Listen. Did you hear it?" she asked.

"Hear what?" he mumbled. "I didn't hear nothing."

"I thought I heard a hound," she muttered.

They stood for a time, but the only thing that came to their ears was the sound of the wind in the trees. Could it be she was weak and losing her mind already, hearing things like folks did when they got lost in the woods? Many times after that he noticed she stopped; just the way she stood, he could tell she was listening for the hound she thought she heard. But no voice of a dog came, and none during the night. Morning, when he looked at her, she lay like a dead person, the baby like a bundle of skin and bone in her arms. Then he saw her stir and watched as incredibly she pulled herself to her feet.

Never would they get far from this place, the boy told himself. Then they both saw what they had failed to see in the darkness when they lay down last night—what looked like a wall of logs hardly a dozen rods off in the forest. They stumbled nearer. It was an old cabin with a roof of bark and a window such as only a white man would make. The cabin stood black, fallen in, and abandoned, but never did any house look so beautiful. Then, as they stood staring at it, they could hear, faint and far away through the morning mist, a sound neither of them could mistake.

"Cowbells!" Mary Harris whispered.

Before noon they reached the river. On the other side they could hear the cowbells more plainly now. To the north, blue pine smoke rose from chimneys among the trees. They took a path under the sycamores till they were across from the settlement. They saw a man fishing on the other side. When they called to him, he dropped his pole and ran. Presently they saw him come back with another man. Both carried guns. They got into a boat. Andy thought they were coming to get them, but the boat moved less than halfway across the water. Here it stopped.

"What do you want?" one of the men called.

"We belong over 'ar. We want to git across."

"You don't look white to us."

"I'm Mary Harris from Black Run."

The two men conferred. "You ain't her. She was took by the Indians."

"I know. I'm just a-gittin' back."

"You ain't Mary Harris. I knowed her. I seed her many a time."

The young woman looked down at herself. As if for the first time, she realized she was half naked, her clothes in shreds, her skin dark with blood and dirt, her hair a tangled mat. She looked forty years old.

"I'm her all right. If you come over, I can prove it."

"No, we ain't comin' nearer. You might have Indian friends in the bushes a-layin' for us."

"Well, if you won't come over, I reckon I'll have to wade out to you the best I can," she said.

"No, it's too deep!" both men called, but she paid no attention. She handed the child to the boy. She warned him sternly not to let her fall. Then she stepped into the water and kept on till it reached her shoulders and threatened to engulf her head.

"Wait!" one man called. "We'll come a mite closer!"

Cautiously the boat edged toward her. Bit by bit, it grew nearer, until the boy heard an exclamation, followed by others. The boat came faster now, and he saw both men lift the dripping woman in. After that they paddled for Andy and the baby, left on the bank.

Boys must have run with the news, for the far bank swarmed with folks by the time the boat touched shore. Before they got there, the older boatman had taken off his hunting shirt that came halfway to his knees and had given it to Mary to hide her nakedness. Now a man on horseback dismounted to let the exhausted woman ride. Against all these well-fed people, she looked little more than a skeleton, and so must he, too, the boy reckoned, for they lifted him up to ride behind her. Over and over, as the people trooped after, he heard them say how never would they have known her.

In the nearest house they put her to bed. Some of the women began pulling thorns from her feet. They counted a hundred and twelve and laid them on a piece of crockery to show. Others of the women had set to cooking. Now it began to smell good. Mary Harris and the young ones had starved a long time, but their empty bellies would get stuffed with rations now.

It was a man they called Major, in small clothes, his hair in a queue, who put a stop to it. He came stamping into the house with his cane and smelled the cookery. "What's this?" he thundered. "You'll kill her! And the boy too! The first day you must give them nothing but whey. One spoonful at a time."

The boy hated him. Others would get the venison stew now. But he hated worse the other man who came bursting in the door after dark. All afternoon Andy had been lying on the bed beside Mary, as he had lain beside her so many nights in the woods, but never had he felt such possession and tenderness for her as now when others tried to come between them. She had fetched him out of the woods. If it hadn't been for her, he would not be here. Her face looked almost like a dead woman's on the bolster, but she needn't worry. Never would he leave her. Soon as he was bigger, he would marry and support her.

He felt outraged and affronted when this stranger came and claimed her as his wife. He hadn't even reckoned on a husband. Why couldn't the Indians have got him like they had so many? But no, here he was putting his rough green-and-blue-linsey arm over Mary Harris's breast and her looking up at him like she had never looked at Andy.

"You leave her alone!" the boy said sharply. When some of the onlookers laughed, he turned his face away.

That laugh burned bitter inside of him. He tried to get up and go off by himself, but they wouldn't let him. All night he lay there hating Mary Harris's man. In the woods he had had her all to himself. Now he must share her with this ugly fellow.

Only Mary Harris's babe gave him comfort. The child knew him, had time for him, played with him a little, pulled and fiddled with his long hair. He looked the babe over with lackluster eyes. Anyway, she wasn't married. She wasn't tied up with any man. Should he want to, he might stake first rights to her. She wasn't much as yet, but she was something. If he couldn't have the mother, he might have the daughter—sometime on ahead when she got old enough to have a man.

The old man came back to the present with a start. Where was he? Oh, yes, here in the mansion office. Well, he did marry the daughter, didn't he? There was her picture hanging on the wall. But it was the woman in the other picture who still stirred him the most. He'd never forget her. She was the one to put iron in a man's soul.

No Rescue

JAMES NORMAN

The airport buildings loomed up out of the night fog like chalk headstones. The taxi came to a halt. The driver turned, giving his fare a questioning glance. "This is Lunatambo."

The man in the back nodded, yet he made no move to get out. He sat within the deep shadows and stared directly ahead, watching the windshield for a telltale reflection. When he was certain no car had followed, he pushed open the door, took his two valises, and hurried across the deserted walk into the airport building.

A drowsy clerk with eyes like lead pellets took his ticket and checked the passenger manifest. "Señor Blanco?"

Edward Duran nodded back.

"They're loading baggage," said the clerk, as he checked Duran's things on the scale. "The flight is in ten minutes. At one forty. You go through the waiting room there."

A ceiling loudspeaker rasped loudly. The Lima, Quito, and Gomera reports. Duran took his ticket and seat slip and went on past the money exchange booths to the waiting room.

A half dozen people were already there, waiting to board the Gomera plane. They stared at Duran when he entered, then reclaimed their glances as though he were not the person they had expected. He nodded at the policeman stationed at the door. Through the big view window facing the field, he saw the shabby C-47, *Aerovias Condor* lettered on its fuselage. The plane was half shrouded in the mist, and shadowy figures of the ground crew moved about it like ants surrounding a wounded dragonfly.

The policeman touched Duran's arm. "There'll be a short delay, *señor*. Please wait here." The man motioned toward the baggage, which had been piled near the outer door, adding, "An inspection."

Duran raised his brows in surprise. "That's not usual?" he asked.

"No, *señor*."

Shrugging, Duran went to one of the leather settees and sat near a middle-aged woman in tweeds, who glanced at him resentfully. He stared briefly at the other passengers, some five or six: a Brazilian general with a deeply cleft chin, who was conversing with a leggy girl who wore a fur cape; a dark-skinned man and his little girl. His attention settled with thoughtful uneasiness upon a young lieutenant in the Montejan Air Force uniform.

A ceiling loudspeaker crackled metallically. "Flight One, Gomera, loading Flight One." The message was repeated in Spanish and English.

A man who walked with ramrod erectness approached the settee. Suddenly the woman beside Duran rose. "Well?" She spoke in an over-loud, annoyed English. "Did you tell the police who we are, Donald?"

The man smiled patiently. An American, Duran decided. But military—perhaps an embassy attaché. Although the man wore civilian clothes, there was about him that brush-stiff bearing that accompanies the professional soldier.

"I spoke to one of them," the man said. "We'll have to wait, dear. But it'll only be a moment."

"Absurd," the woman replied petulantly. "Didn't you show our papers?"

The man nodded. "They're making a special check," he replied. "Doing it on all the flights from and to Gomera. Semi-civil-war situation there. Lot of people slipping back and forth who shouldn't be. Illegal papers and all that."

Duran sat motionless, and although he showed nothing outwardly, his body tingled as if some violent shock had been transmitted through his heels. He heard the man's voice a long way off: "Too many of these comic-opera upsets down here. Hard to keep up on them. Somebody gets in the government, his cousins don't like him—pooft—civil war for a few days."

Duran tried to shut off the voice. He had an impulse to get up and walk away, to get out upon the dark, mist-shrouded field and run. He glanced toward the door and, abruptly, his heart sank.

Two Peruvian officials and a man in mufti had come in.

He had only to glimpse the latter—a squarish, comfortably built man with a moustache the shape of two well-milled pennies—and he knew that the trouble he had not expected, so soon, had come. The man was a Montejan. From Gomera. He knew his face and feared it.

The three men went to the corner where the baggage had been assembled. One of the officials called out a name from the passenger list, "Señorita Tovar? Please, over here." The girl with the fur cape stood up.

While they inspected her papers and baggage, Duran's eyes made a restless circuit of the room. Now, even if he wanted to, he couldn't run. Both entrances were guarded. He glanced cautiously toward the penny-moustache man. The latter wore a self-effacing black suit and a high celluloid collar three sizes too large for his neck. It seemed purposely that way, perhaps to create an impression of ridiculousness or to divert attention from his eyes, which gave his character away. His eyes were like black impersonal seals, which had a way of reaching forth, planting themselves on someone, and sticking like postage stamps.

The man's name was Rozas—Rozas, of the Montejan Special Police. Among newsmen in Gomera, and the countless Montejans who had had the temerity to object to the dictatorship there, which had gradually strangled the press and free elections, he was known as El Godo, or the Goth.

"Señor Blanco, please."

Duran jerked to attention. He saw that Rozas's black eyes had settled upon him and stuck. As he crossed the room he slipped his faked Argentine passport and papers from his pocket. They've got to be good, he prayed. They've got to get me through.

One of the Peruvian officials scrutinized the papers carefully, then turned them over to Rozas. The latter didn't open
the passport. He weighed it delicately in his hand as though
judging its age and use by its feel. His eyes were still stuck
against Duran. Then, for an instant, they flicked toward
one of the Peruvians.

"One meter eighty in height," Rozas commented. "Weight,
seventy kilos, eh? Brown eyes. Sharp, bony nose. The hair is
not the same. Too dark now. And his eyebrows are changed.
There is also this moustache." He smiled for a second, then
his smile burned out. "So you call yourself Señor Blanco now,
eh, Duran?"

Inwardly, Duran steeled himself. Was it that Rozas had
readily probed through the changes he had so carefully made
upon himself? Or did they suspect the forged passport? He
looked at Rozas and the officials, and assumed a confused
expression. "What did you say?" he asked in Spanish.

"Your name?" Rozas shifted to Spanish also.

"It's there." Duran pointed to the passport. "I'm Carlos
Blanco."

Rozas glanced at one of the Peruvians. "He fits the description, but for some changes," he said. "Under the changes,
perhaps we have the American, Duran."

The Peruvian official, a dour, sleepy man, stared at Duran.
"When did you enter Peru?"

"Three days ago," Duran replied.

"From where? Montejo? Gomera?"

"No. From Bolivia, La Paz. Before that Buenos Aires. I
came by air. You can check last week's incoming passenger
lists here."

"Your business?"

"Selling."

The official motioned for him to open his valises. Rozas crouched over the small sample case, fingering through the stock of plastic Swiss hearing aids. He took an inordinately long time, clucking over the descriptive booklets, thumbing through the order blanks. Then he turned to the other valise and picked over the labels on Duran's garments.

Duran smiled faintly. They were not sure, he thought with relief. They were not sure. They knew only as much as you or someone else told them. The clothing labels, the passport, the order blanks would tell them nothing. He thanked God he had been so thorough in preparing the part he had to play. There were labels to match the counterfeit visas on his passport—Venezuelan, Brazilian, Bolivian. And in the order books there were carbons of orders for hearing aids he had actually managed to contract for with merchandisers like Casa Grace, Wiesse, and Duncan Fox.

Rozas sighed and stood up. He glanced at Duran bleakly. "Such detail. Such observance of little detail," he observed.

Duran's senses froze over. Perhaps he had done it too thoroughly. Perhaps Rozas had begun to think he was part of some elaborate underground outfit. The urge returned to break and run. Then, to his surprise, Rozas motioned for the valise to be shut and gave an indifferent shrug.

"There's the likeness," Rozas said to the Peruvian, "but he's not the one."

The stewardess showed him his place and gave him a blanket. He watched through the window as the passengers came, one by one, toward the plane. The American and his caustic-voiced wife were among the last.

"Why should they be looking for an American?" Her voice filled the cabin corridor.

Duran looked up, his eyes meeting those of the American man. The latter looked down with a cold curiosity, nodded briefly, and went on to his seat. Duran peered uneasily through the window again.

The long necklace of strip lights had blinked on, extending dimly in the fog. In the cabin ahead, the pilot took the signal from the tower and the prewarmed engines picked up a throaty roar. The plane waddled out to the runway and turned slowly. Duran heard the murmur of voices behind him, then saw the stewardess come through, checking safety belts. He sat back and, for the first time, began to relax.

He glanced at his watch. It was two o'clock. Four hours until dawn. That would put the plane approximately over the Peruvian-Montejan frontier. Then another two hours or so to Gomera. The distance was not great in air miles, but detours had to be made to avoid the towering Andean peaks that thumbed icy fingers into the sky.

Just as the engines outside burst into an angry roar and the plane thundered up the strip, a man hurried from the rear and slid into the seat across from Duran. For an instant, Duran stared with abrupt, sickening shock. The man was Rozas.

His heart drummed at the base of his skull as he withdrew his gaze. He tried to think reasonably, to overcome the waves of fear. Rozas was following him; this much was obvious. A new fear stirred within him, welling up quickly. A cat-and-mouse thing. Rozas was waiting, expecting him to contact someone in Gomera. How, now, was he going to reach Anna Maria, Duran thought desperately.

He shut his eyes and forced an uncertain calm upon himself. Still, it was no use. Behind the darkness of his lids he felt the throb of the engines pulling the plane up through the coastal fog, up the lone climb out of Lima's fanlike Rimac Valley, and out over the high, mist-veiled Andes. He could hear the murmur of other passengers' voices, and he sensed Rozas's eyes sticking against him.

Sounds, memories from beyond the plane flooded in upon him: vivid remembrances of escape down from the snow-crested Montejan highlands, into the Cartagenan jungle, across its tobacco-colored rivers, and then the months of moving through the high gray grass of the Montejan plains, fleeing from one village to another. And always, hovering behind the memories of hardships, the image of Anna Maria, his wife, in Gomera. The last night, taking leave of her there. The shocked look in her eyes when she had learned that the police wanted him, that there was a price on his head.

Months had dissolved without a word from her. He had been unable to write for fear of getting her into trouble. Her family were Army people, her father a general, the kind who remained aloof from governmental squabbles. During the lonely nights he had dreamed only of getting word to her that she should join him in Venezuela. Then one day there had been a message, word brought down by a news correspondent whose offices had also been closed by El Godo's men.

Anna Maria couldn't come to him. The police had refused her the necessary exit papers, and they were watching her. He had become afraid that the police might arrest her to find out where he was. They would never believe that she wasn't in communication with him. Knowing this, there was nothing to do but risk going in himself, finding her, and escaping with her as he had once before escaped. She couldn't do it alone. It was too dangerous. But if he went back, there were ways, and there were people who could help. Not always the best people, but if you knew the ropes and paid enough. . . .

He had gradually made his way to Argentina, managed to buy a faked identity card, changed his features somewhat. Now he was heading back.

He opened his eyes slightly and glanced sidewise at Rozas. The latter was asleep or feigning sleep. His black fedora was smashed over his face. He clutched a briefcase on his lap.

Duran was suddenly conscious of the plane winging through the chilled darkness at fifteen thousand feet. Escape lay below, not too far below on those cold bleak Andean highlands, only a step down from the snow and glacier belt. Still, there was no escape. How was he going to reach Anna Maria? Unless, possibly, he could bluff it through? Or make a run for it at the airport? Impossible. There would be not only El Godo; some of his men would be waiting.

He considered this bitterly. It would be the end of the meeting that could never take place. The reunion he had so longed for, had built up in detail within his heart, inch by inch, moment by moment, during the past year.

Hours of flight brought calmness to him, an almost fatalistic acceptance of things as they were. He became aware of the atmosphere in the plane, a faint tension. The stewardess had gone forward to the pilot's compartment and had come out with a worried setness to her lips. Outside, although it was almost dawn, there was no visibility below. A clammy mist had erased the earth. Duran sensed that they had been driven off course.

He was about to call the stewardess when he saw Rozas looking at him. "Please." Rozas spoke so his voice came barely above the sound of the engines. "You have had time to think, eh? Would it ease your mind if it were arranged that you are not arrested when we land?"

Duran stared back without emotion. He had become almost accustomed to the tight sensation in his chest, the rapid hammering of his heart, that came when his eyes met those of the other man. "There's some mistake," he countered. "I don't understand."

"No mistake." Rozas shook his head. "No mistake, Señor Duran."

Duran shrugged.

"Simply because there are no fingerprints"—Rozas paused, smiling faintly—"it does not mean we don't know you, *señor*. There is the Eduardo, or Edward—which do you prefer?— the Eduardo Duran who was brought up in Ecuador, but whose father was American. Also there is the Duran who studied in the United States. Cal Tech, they call it, yes? Radio. This one returned to Latin America and he married in Gomera. A Montejan girl."

Duran's face remained a mask, yet his nerves were throbbing like taut, plucked wires.

"This Duran," Rozas went on, "had something to do with a foreign press. A radio news service, yes?"

Duran shook his head. But for an instant his thoughts flashed back: a memory of Gomera under the dictatorship. When the government, if you could call it that, had seized a number of newspapers—some old and very respected ones —and had clamped down on the foreign correspondents, he had resisted it. When the press-radio outfit he worked for had been shut down, he had risked building a clandestine sender to get the news out for American and Latin-American correspondents.

One night there had been a police raid. A police informer had been killed. Neither Duran nor the two foreign correspondents with him at the time had had guns. Yet they had framed a murder charge against him—a handy club the police could hold over his head.

"The police might overlook certain events," Rozas's voice broke in on his thoughts. "You can be of help, and at liberty. . . ."

Duran frowned. He knew that Rozas was fishing. There had been others involved in the construction of the radio sender, others who were still in Gomera. He had had the backing of some of the top publishers. The frame-up was part of it, a club to make him reveal the others. "Look," he said with controlled annoyance, "my name is Carlos Blanco! I've never heard of this man you're talking about."

Rozas's neck swiveled in its overlarge collar. The man leaned forward almost confidentially. "*Señor*, there's no use hiding. You'll be identified at the airport when we land. You'll be identified by your wife."

Duran's thoughts froze abruptly. Anna Maria! They had taken her. Then Rozas's voice came through the barrier of shock, "I wired from Lima. Over an hour ago your wife was informed by a person she trusts, a former friend of yours, that you're coming in. She'll be at the airport. Naturally she doesn't know she'll be observed."

The emotion of shock thawed away. Duran had a sudden desire to smash his knuckles into the man's round face. Controlling himself, he shook his head, as though he were still

Carlos Blanco. He half opened his mouth in answer to Rozas when he saw the Montejan Air Force lieutenant in the seat ahead turn and glance back worriedly.

"The engine . . ." said the lieutenant, pointing outside.

Duran turned to the window, grateful for the excuse to turn away from Rozas. He rubbed the mist from the pane and cupped his hands to peer out. The plane had broken through the blanket of fog. He caught a glimpse of mist streamers, of snow and soaring mountain peaks, all much too close for comfort. Then he became conscious of the putter and death of one of the engines. The howl of the slipstream seemed louder and chilling.

He glanced toward the lieutenant, saying, "Mountains! We're too low!"

The stewardess hurried down the corridor, warning the passengers to fasten safety belts. There was a babble of strained voices as Duran cupped his hand to the window again. Suddenly his breath left him under the sharp blow-like straining of his safety belt. At the same instant there was a driving roar and crash. An engine outside bellowed, then silenced. In a blur, Duran saw the stewardess sail down the corridor and smash against the door of the pilot's compartment.

He tore at his belt, broke free, and scrambled up the tilting corridor to the rear door, the thought of fire driving him as he kicked the door open. Behind him came panic-stricken voices and someone's piercing scream. He caught twisted glimpses: the stewardess and someone else crumpled on the floor, the Montejan lieutenant leaning drunkenly against a seat, and Rozas slumped over, held like a sack by his safety belt.

Through the open door there was a brief expanse of white. Wind whipped the snow in lashing banners. The nose of the plane was half buried in snow, which had broken the shock of the crash. For a moment Duran stared out as though mesmerized. The snow line! A long step below it lay the bleak, wind-swept highlands and an offer of escape.

Someone in the corridor behind him moaned pitifully. He glanced back and saw a few of the passengers stumbling about.

The lieutenant came up beside Duran. "No fire," he muttered hoarsely.

Duran nodded. He stared out at the snow, and after a moment of hesitation he slowly pulled the door shut. He motioned to the lieutenant to help him with the passengers.

There was plenty to do. The dark-skinned man lay in the aisle. He breathed shallowly and a flow of blood ran down his face. A child, his daughter, clung to him, screaming hysterically. The American passenger was holding his wife, who seemed to be unconscious, while at the same time the Brazilian general was bracing himself to stand on the slanting floor. His right arm hung limply. Duran leaned over the Peruvian girl. She seemed unhurt, but suffering from shock.

Duran and the lieutenant, whose name was Vidal, went among the passengers, quieting them, giving aid. They moved the man from the aisle onto a stretcher and braced it at a better angle. Fractured skull, Duran guessed, but he couldn't tell how serious it was. The stewardess was as badly off. Her breath came in gasps from her crushed lungs.

Vidal brought the first-aid kit, and Duran emptied morphine into the girl and the injured man. He lifted the child, who now wept inconsolably, and holding her gently, murmured, "He'll be all right. We'll take came of him the best we can." He turned to the American, whose wife had regained consciousness and seemed better. He asked them to watch the child. As he spoke to them in Spanish, he saw that Rozas, too, had recovered. El Godo sat in his place, dazedly fumbling with the safety belt.

From the front of the passage, Lieutenant Vidal motioned to him. "Pilot and copilot are dead," the lieutenant murmured. "Come."

Duran followed him into the compartment. The place was a shambles of broken glass, smashed instrument panels, and twisted metal. Snow whipped in from the broken window. "Not much warning for them," said Vidal. Duran nodded, glancing at the dead pilot. His face was hardly recognizable as a face. The copilot bore no marks of injury, but he was gone too.

"Better put them outside," Duran said.

When Duran and the lieutenant returned to the passenger compartment, a certain normality had replaced the air of confusion. The American woman held the child on her lap, comforting her. Her husband had managed to make coffee and pass it around. Señorita Tovar was hovering over the seriously injured passengers, who had been moved to the rear of the compartment. In addition to blankets, her fur cape had been laid over the stewardess.

The American served Duran and Vidal cups of steaming black coffee. "My name is Kemp, Colonel Kemp," he said in his stiff, correct Spanish. "I want to thank you both. Capable work."

The Brazilian general nodded in agreement. "Do you have any idea where we are?" he asked.

Duran glanced at Vidal. The young officer shrugged. "In the Andes," he said. "But where? Who knows?"

"Any chance of rescue?" asked the American colonel.

"Possibly the copilot got a message off," Duran said. "If he did, they'll be searching right away. But the lieutenant says we're pretty far off course. Might be days before they find us."

As he spoke he noticed Rozas. The man watched with those stamplike eyes, and he seemed to hold apart from the others.

"Radio?" asked Colonel Kemp.

"It's smashed," replied Lieutenant Vidal. "I know radio, but not enough to fix this one, the condition it's in."

Duran saw Rozas lean forward and moisten his lips. Now he felt it coming, felt it in the way Rozas moved and the manner in which he had been watching the passengers.

"It can be repaired," said Rozas. The others looked at him hopefully.

"Señor Duran is a radio engineer, an excellent one," Rozas went on. "But he insists he isn't Duran. This is natural, for he is wanted by the police. He doesn't wish to expose himself." Rozas paused, smiling bleakly. "Perhaps if he were assured there would be no arrest. . . ."

Duran felt the curiosity of the others upon him now. For the moment, this didn't trouble him. He thought of the radio. There was a possibility that it could be repaired. A thin possibility. Then he thought of Anna Maria waiting at the airport, and of the police there. He stared at Rozas, and suddenly he had the feeling that Rozas didn't really care whether the radio was fixed, whether help came quickly for the injured, or in a few days. The trap Rozas had expected to spring at the airport had crashed with the plane. Now Rozas was probing again. He wanted to be sure.

Without looking at the others, Duran turned, made his way up the corridor, and stood near the Peruvian girl as she watched over the injured passengers. He knelt beside her and felt the stewardess's pulse. It was weak.

"They need a doctor," Señorita Tovar murmured.

He nodded silently. Then he rose, went back to the baggage section, and found his sample case. When he reappeared, Rozas was waiting alertly, as though prepared to pursue him. Duran nodded toward the front and gave Lieutenant Vidal a faint smile.

"We'll try the radio," he said.

Vidal dug out the plane's repair kit and spare parts. He shook his head. "Perhaps there aren't enough tubes," he said.

"I know," Duran replied. "We'll try transistors, if necessary. Will you check the battery? We'll need power."

He took stock of the transmitter. Now, for an hour, he and Vidal crimped wires, traced out circuits, removed the tiny transistors from Duran's hearing aids, and were able to use some of them. They tested, crimped, and checked until their fingers were numbed by the high Andean cold. Once during their work, the lieutenant paused, looking over what had been assembled.

Then he glanced at Duran, asking, "It's true then? You're this Duran?"

Duran nodded. "Does it trouble you?"

The lieutenant hesitated. "We have no opinions in the Army."

"Some of the Army has been hunting me too," Duran said grimly.

The young officer shrugged. Jerking his head toward the passenger compartment, he said, "The Army takes orders. But we're tired of those like El Godo. Perhaps the Army, too, loses patience with those who do not believe in democracy."

Colonel Kemp brought coffee to the cold, battered pilot's compartment. As he handed Duran a cup, he looked at him questioningly. "American?" he asked in English.

Duran smiled thinly. "My home is here," he replied. "My wife too."

"I won't ask what your trouble is."

"You can."

The colonel shrugged. His face was quite expressionless. He stared down at the radio and, after a moment, asked, "Is it going to work?"

"It may. Perhaps we can raise Gomera or one of the military fields. Flor or Salar. We'll be operating on battery. Not much power."

Duran turned to the set, made a final check, and tried sending. He made another adjustment. Finally he raised a weak signal. The field at Gomera. He reported the crash tersely. The field replied that an air search had already begun. They'd send a plane to drop medical supplies, food, blankets, and possibly parachute in an Army doctor. He was ordered to signal briefly at intervals, so that they could get a triangulation.

A few minutes later the field shot back the triangulation report. Their plane had crashed in the Cordillera Oriental, just inside the Montejan border. It was desolate country and a ground-rescue party would have trouble getting to them. Leaving Lieutenant Vidal to maintain interval contact with the field, Duran went to the passenger compartment to give them the news.

As he stepped into the compartment he was startled by the silence and the stiffness upon the faces before him. Then, in a single swift glance, he saw Rozas sitting apart from the others. There was a .45 automatic on his lap and the glint of handcuffs upon his knee.

Duran stared at him impassively. It was Colonel Kemp who stirred first. He turned toward Rozas, speaking in irritation, "No need for this, man. He could have escaped and taken his chances in the mountains when we crashed."

"He didn't," Rozas replied. "That was his mistake."

"You don't intend to handcuff him in this cold?" It was the colonel's wife who spoke.

Rozas shrugged. "I don't intend to have him escape."

"But you said, if he fixed the radio. . . ."

The woman's angry charge was interrupted as Lieutenant Vidal entered the compartment. For a second, Vidal stood stiffly, looking at Duran and Rozas.

"What it it?" Duran asked him.

Vidal hesitated. "Gomera wants a list of the injured and the passengers," he said.

Rozas signaled to the lieutenant. "First, Lieutenant, I have a message for you to radio."

Vidal stared at him coldly. "The passenger list," he said.

Rozas's hand tightened upon his gun. Then he shrugged, saying, "Yes, the list. Put down my name, Antonio Rozas, M.S.S. Then Eduardo Duran, prisoner."

Vidal looked at the American colonel. "Yours, *señor?*"

The colonel glanced at Rozas with a peculiar intentness. Then his attention flicked toward the rear of the compart-

ment. The others around him became abruptly conscious of
the gasping breath of the stewardess and the moans from
the child's father.

Looking at Vidal, the colonel said, "My name's Duran.
Edward Duran."

"Duran?" The lieutenant repeated it, startled.

"Duran! That's it," the colonel replied brusquely.

The Brazilian general seated behind the Americans motioned with his uninjured hand. "I am Duran too. General
Eduardo Duran."

"Duran, here," cut in the American woman. "And the
child here, her name is. . . ."

Rozas had started to rise, clutching the ugly black automatic and the handcuffs. The cuffs slipped from his fingers
and clattered on the floor, skating down toward Duran.
Rozas's eyes followed them with a stunned expression. When
he looked at the passengers again, it was as though he were
facing a forbidding wall of cold eyes. Even the Montejan
lieutenant, whom he might have counted upon, now stood
beside Duran as though he, too, were a part of the man.

Rozas sank back into his seat slowly. His fingers fumbled
with the flap of his briefcase and he slid the gun inside,
hiding it.

The high, taut voice of the wind had dulled Duran's alert-
ness as he made his way slowly down the jagged glacial
moraine. He didn't hear the drone of the search plane until
it had passed over him. Looking up, he shaded his eyes from
the glare and spied the plane above the serrated snow peaks.

It circled high and to the left above the narrow mountain
shelf where, two miles away, the C-47's dark tail and rudder

assembly protruded above the snow like a feathered shaft. He watched the plane make one pass, then slowly circle for another. A colored chute blossomed from beneath the search plane and drifted petallike toward the crash area.

Although he knew that the people up there on the mountain shelf were watching the chute, nevertheless he raised his arm and waved. A sense of warmth welled up within him as he thought of the lieutenant, the Brazilian general with the cleft chin, and the others up there. Then he shouldered his pack—the blanket, chocolate squares, the flask of brandy, and the pistol—which the colonel and his wife had insisted he take along. He turned, and as he continued on his way down the tortuous sweep of mountains he knew now that he would be able to reach Anna Maria and get her out of the country.

Freedom's a Hard-bought Thing

STEPHEN VINCENT BENÉT

A long time ago, in times gone by, in slavery times, there was a man named Cue. I want you to think about him. I've got a reason. He got born like the cotton in the boll or the rabbit in the pea patch. There wasn't any fine doings when he got born, but his mammy was glad to have him. Yes. He didn't get born in the Big House, or the overseer's house, or any place where the bearing was easy or the work light. No, Lord. He came out of his mammy in a field-hand's cabin one sharp winter, and about the first thing he remembered was his mammy's face and the taste of a piece of bacon rind and the light and shine of the pitch-pine fire up the chimney. Well, now, he got born and there he was.

His daddy worked in the fields, and his mammy worked in the fields when she wasn't bearing. They were slaves; they chopped the cotton and hoed the corn. They heard the horn blow before the light came and the horn blow that meant the day's work was done. His daddy was a strong man, strong in his back and strong in his arms. The white folks called him Cuffee. His mammy was a good woman, yes, Lord. The white folks called her Sarah, and she was gentle with her hands and gentle with her voice. She had a voice like the river going by in the night, and at night when she wasn't too tired she'd sing songs to little Cue. Some had foreign words in them—African words. She couldn't remember what some of them meant, but they'd come to her down out of time.

Now, how am I going to describe and explain about that time when that time's gone? The white folks lived in the Big House, and they had many to tend on them. Old Marster, he lived there like Pharaoh and Solomon, mighty splendid and fine. He had his flocks and his herds, his butler and his baker; his fields ran from the river to the woods and back again. He'd ride around the fields each day on his big horse, Black Billy, just like thunder and lightning, and evenings he'd sit at his table and drink his wine. Man, that was a sight to see, with all the silver knives and the silver forks, the glass decanters, and the gentlemen and ladies from all over. It was a sight to see. When Cue was young, it seemed to him that Old Marster must own the whole world, right up to the edge of the sky.

There were things that changed on the plantation, but it didn't change. There were bad times and good times. There was the time young Marse Edward got bit by the snake, and the time Big Rambo ran away and they caught him with the dogs and brought him back. There was a swivel-eyed overseer that beat folks too much, and then there was Mr. Wade, and he wasn't so bad. There was hog-killing time and Christmas and springtime and summertime. Cue didn't wonder about it or why things happened that way; he didn't expect it to be different. A bee in a hive don't ask you how there come to be a hive in the beginning. Cue grew up strong; he grew up smart with his hands. They put him in the blacksmith shop to help Daddy Jake; he didn't like it, at first, because Daddy Jake was mighty cross-tempered. Then he got to like the work; he learned to forge iron and shape it; he learned to shoe a horse and tire a wagon wheel, and everything a blacksmith does. One time they let him shoe Black Billy, and he shod him light and tight and Old Marster praised him in front of Mr. Wade. He was strong; he was black as night; he was proud of his back and his arms.

Now he might have stayed that way, yes, he might. He heard freedom talk, now and then, but he didn't pay much mind to it. He wasn't a talker or a preacher; he was Cue and he worked in the blacksmith shop. He didn't want to be a field hand, but he didn't want to be a house servant either. He'd rather be Cue than poor white trash or owned by poor white trash. That's the way he felt; I'm obliged to tell the truth about that way.

Then there was a sickness came and his mammy and his daddy died of it. Old Miss got the doctor for them, but they died just the same. After that, Cue felt lonesome.

He felt lonesome and troubled in his mind. He'd seen his daddy and his mammy put in the ground and new slaves come to take their cabin. He didn't repine about that, because he knew things had to be that way. But when he went to bed at night in the loft over the blacksmith shop, he'd keep thinking about his mammy and his daddy—how strong his daddy was and the songs that his mammy sang. They'd worked all their lives and had children, though he was the only one left, but the only place of their own they had was the place in the burying ground. And yet they'd been good and faithful servants, because Old Marster said so, with his hat off, when he buried them. The Big House stayed, and the cotton and the corn, but Cue's mammy and daddy were gone like last year's crop. It made Cue wonder, and it troubled him.

He began to take notice of things he'd never noticed. When the horn blew in the morning for the hands to go to the fields, he'd wonder who started blowing that horn in the first place. It wasn't like thunder and lightning; somebody had started it. When he heard Old Marster say, when he was talking to a friend, "This damned epidemic! It's cost me eight prime field hands and the best-trained butler in the state. I'd rather have lost the Flyaway colt than Old Isaac," Cue put that down in his mind and pondered it. Old Marster didn't mean it mean, and he'd sat up with Old Isaac all night before he died. But Isaac and Cue and the Flyaway colt, they all belonged to Old Marster and he owned them, hide and hair. He owned them, like money in his pockets. Well, Cue had known that all his life, but because he was troubled now, it gave him a queer feeling.

Well, now, he was shoeing a horse for young Marster

Shepley one day, and he shod it light and tight. And when
he was through he made a stirrup for young Marster Shepley,
and young Marster Shepley mounted and threw him a silver
bit with a laughing word. That shouldn't have bothered Cue,
because gentlemen sometimes did that. And Old Marster
wasn't mean; he didn't object. But all night Cue kept feeling
the print of young Marster Shepley's heel in his hands. And
yet he liked young Marster Shepley. He couldn't explain it
at all.

Finally Cue decided he must be conjured. He didn't know
who had done it or why they'd done it. But he knew what
he had to do. He had to go see Aunt Rachel.

Aunt Rachel was an old, old woman, and she lived in a
cabin by herself with her granddaughter Sukey. She'd seen
Old Marster's father and his father, and the tale went she'd
seen George Washington with his hair all white, and General Lafayette in his gold-plated suit of clothes that the king
of France gave him to fight in. Some folks said she was a
conjure and some folks said she wasn't, but everybody on
the plantation treated her mighty respectful, because, if she
put her eye on you, she mightn't take it off. Well, his mammy
had been friends with Aunt Rachel, so Cue went to see her.

She was sitting alone in her cabin by the low light of a
fire. There was a pot on the fire, and now and then you
could hear it bubble and chunk, like a bullfrog chunking
in the swamp, but that was the only sound. Cue made his
obleegances to her and asked her about the misery in her
back. Then he gave her a chicken he happened to bring along.
It was a black rooster, and she seemed pleased to get it. She
took it in her thin black hands, and it fluttered and clucked
a minute. So she drew a chalk line from its beak along a

board, and then it stayed still and frozen. Well, Cue had seen that trick done before. But it was different, seeing it done in Aunt Rachel's cabin, with the big pot chunking on the fire. It made him feel uneasy, and he jingled the bit in his pocket for company.

After a while the old woman spoke. "Well, Son Cue," said she, "that's a fine young rooster you've brought me. What else did you bring me, Son Cue?"

"I brought you trouble," said Cue in a husky voice, because that was all he could think of to say.

She nodded her head as if she'd expected that. "They mostly brings me trouble," she said. "They mostly brings trouble to Aunt Rachel. What kind of trouble, Son Cue? Man trouble or woman trouble?"

"It's my trouble," said Cue, and he told her the best way he could. When he'd finished, the pot on the fire gave a bubble and a croak, and the old woman took a long spoon and stirred it.

"Well, Son Cue, son of Cuffee, son of Shango," she said. "You've got a big trouble for sure."

"Is it going to kill me dead?" said Cue.

"I can't tell you right about that," said Aunt Rachel. "I could give you lies and prescriptions. Maybe I would, to some folks. But your granddaddy Shango was a powerful man. It took three men to put the irons on him, and I saw the irons break his heart. I won't lie to you, Son Cue. You've got a sickness."

"Is it a bad sickness?" said Cue.

"It's a sickness in your blood," said Aunt Rachel. "It's a sickness in your liver and your veins. Your daddy never had it that I knows of. He took after his mammy's side. But his daddy was a Corromantee, and they is bold and free, and you takes after him. It's the freedom sickness, Son Cue."

"The freedom sickness?" said Cue.

"The freedom sickness," said the old woman, and her little eyes glittered like sparks. "Some they break and some they tame down," she said, "and some is neither to be tamed or broken. Don't I know the signs and the sorrow—me that come through the middle passage on the slavery ship and seen my folks scattered like sand? Ain't I seen it coming, Lord? O Lord, ain't I seen it coming?"

"What's coming?" said Cue.

"A darkness in the sky and a cloud with a sword in it," said the old woman, stirring the pot, "because they hold our people, and they hold our people."

Cue began to tremble. "I don't want to get whipped," he said. "I never been whipped, not hard."

"They whipped your granddaddy Shango till the blood ran twinkling down his back," said the old woman, "but some you can't break or tame."

"I don't want to be chased by dogs," said Cue. "I don't want to hear the dogs belling and the paterollers after me."

The old woman stirred the pot.

"Old Marster, he's a good marster," said Cue. "I don't want to do him no harm. I don't want no trouble or projecting to get me into trouble."

The old woman stirred the pot and stirred the pot.

"O God, I want to be free," said Cue. "I just ache and hone to be free. How I going to be free, Aunt Rachel?"

"There's a road that runs underground," said the old woman. "I never seen it, but I knows of it. There's a railroad train that runs, sparking and snorting, underground through the earth. At least, that's what they tell me. But I wouldn't know for sure." She looked at Cue.

Cue looked back at her bold enough, for he'd heard about the Underground Railroad himself, just mentions and whispers. But he knew there wasn't any use asking the old woman what she wouldn't tell. "How I going to find that road, Aunt Rachel?" he said.

"You look at the rabbit in the brier and you see what it do. You look at the owl in the woods and you see what it do. You look at the star in the sky and you see what she do. Then you come back and talk to me. Now I'm going to eat, because I'm hungry."

That was all the words she'd say to him that night, but when Cue went back to his loft, her words kept boiling around in his mind. All night he could hear that train of railroad cars snorting and sparking underground through the earth. So, next morning, he ran away.

He didn't run far or fast. How could he? He'd never been more than twenty miles from the plantation in his life; he didn't know the roads or the ways. He ran off before the horn, and Mr. Wade caught him before sundown. Now wasn't he a stupid man, that Cue?

When they brought him back Mr. Wade let him off light, because he was a good boy and never had run away before. All the same, he got ten, and ten laid over the ten. Yellow Joe, the head driver, laid them on. The first time the whip cut into him it was like a fire on Cue's skin, and he didn't see how he could stand it. Then he got to a place where he could.

After it was over Aunt Rachel crope up to his loft and had her granddaughter Sukey put salve on his back. Sukey, she was sixteen, and golden skinned and pretty as a peach on a peach tree. She worked in the Big House, and he never expected her to do a thing like that.

"I'm mighty obliged," he said, though he kept thinking it was Aunt Rachel got him into trouble and he didn't feel as obliged as he might.

"Is that all you've got to say to me, Son Cue?" said Aunt Rachel, looking down at him. "I told you to watch three things. Did you watch them?"

"No'm," said Cue. "I run off in the woods just like I was a wild turkey. I won't never do that no more."

"You're right, Son Cue," said the old woman. "Freedom's a hard-bought thing. So, now you've been whipped, I reckon you'll give it up."

"I been whipped," said Cue, "but there's a road running underground. You told me so. I been whipped, but I ain't beaten."

"Now you're learning a thing to remember," said Aunt Rachel, and went away. But Sukey stayed behind for a while and cooked Cue's supper. He never expected her to do a thing like that, but he liked it when she did.

When his back got healed, they put him with the field gang for a while. But then there was blacksmith work that needed to be done, and they put him back in the blacksmith shop. And things went on for a long time just the way they had before. But there was a difference in Cue. It was like he'd lived up till now with his ears and his eyes sealed over. And now he began to open his eyes and his ears.

He looked at the rabbit in the brier, and he saw it could hide. He looked at the owl in the woods, and he saw it went soft through the night. He looked at the star in the sky, and he saw she pointed north. Then he began to figure.

He couldn't figure things fast, so he had to figure things slow. He figured the owl and the rabbit got wisdom the white folks don't know about. But he figured the white folks got wisdom he don't know about. They got reading and writing wisdom, and it seem mighty powerful. He asked Aunt Rachel if that's so, and she say it's so.

That's how come he learned to read and write. He ain't supposed to. But Sukey, she learned some of that wisdom, along with the young misses, and she teach him out of a little book she tote from the Big House. The little book, it's all about bats and rats and cats, and Cue figured whoever wrote it must be sort of touched in the head not to write about things folks would want to know, instead of all those trifling animals. But he put himself to it and he learned. It almost bust his head, but he learn. It's a proud day for him when he write his name, "Cue," in the dust with the end of a stick, and Sukey tell him that's right.

Now he began to hear the first rumblings of that train running underground—that train that's the Underground Railroad. Oh, children, remember the names of Levi Coffin and John Hansen! Remember the Quaker saints that hid the fugitive! Remember the names of all those that helped set our people free!

There's a word dropped here and a word dropped there and a word that's passed around. Nobody know where the word come from or where it goes, but it's there. There's many a word spoken in the quarters that the Big House never hears about. There's a heap said in front of the fire that never flies up the chimney. There's a name you tell to the grapevine that the grapevine don't tell back.

There was a white man, one day, came by selling maps and pictures. The quality folks, they looked at his maps and pictures, and he talked with them mighty pleasant and respectful. But while Cue was tightening a bolt on his wagon he dropped a word and a word. The word he said made that underground train come nearer.

Cue met the man one night, all alone, in the woods. He's a quiet man with a thin face. He hold his life in his hands every day he walk about, but he don't make nothing of that. Cue's seen bold folks and bodacious folks, but it's the first time he's seen a man bold that way. It make him proud to be a man. The man ask Cue questions, and Cue give him answers. While he's seeing that man Cue don't just think about himself anymore. He think about all his people that's in trouble.

The man say something to him, he say, "No man own the earth. It's too big for one man." He say, "No man own another man, that's too big a thing too." Cue think about those words and ponder them. But when he gets back to his loft, the courage drains out of him and he sits on his straw tick, staring at the wall. That's the time the darkness comes to him and the shadow falls on him.

He aches and he hones for freedom, but he aches and he hones for Sukey too. And Lot Ti's cabin is empty, and it's a good cabin. All he's got to do is to go to Old Marster and take Sukey with him. Old Marster don't approve to mix the field hand with the house servant, but Cue's different; Cue's a blacksmith. He can see the way Sukey would look, coming back to her in the evening. He can see the way she'd be in the morning before the horn. He can see all that. It ain't freedom, but it's what he's used to. And the other way's long and hard and lonesome and strange.

"O Lord, why you put this burden on a man like me?" say Cue. Then he listen a long time for the Lord to tell him, and it seem to him, at last, that he get an answer. The answer ain't in any words, but it's a feeling in his heart.

So when the time come and the plan ripe and they get to the boat on the river and they see there's one too many for the boat, Cue know the answer. He don't have to hear the quiet white man say, "There's one too many for the boat." He just pitch Sukey into it before he can think too hard. He don't say a word or a groan. He know it's that way and there's bound to be a reason for it. He stand on the bank in the dark and see the boat pull away, like Israel's children. Then he hear the shouts and the shot. He know what he's bound to do then, and the reason for it. He know it's the paterollers, and he show himself. When he get back to the plantation he's worn and tired. But the paterollers, they've chased him instead of the boat.

He creep by Aunt Rachel's cabin and he see the fire at her window. So he scratch at the door and go in. And there she is, sitting by the fire, all hunched up and little.

"You looks poorly, Son Cue," she say when he come in, though she don't take her eye off the pot.

"I'm poorly, Aunt Rachel," he say. "I'm sick and sorry and distressed."

"What's the mud on your jeans, Son Cue?" she say, and the pot, it bubble and croak.

"That's the mud of the swamp where I hid from the paterollers," he say.

"What's the hole in your leg, Son Cue?" she say, and the pot, it croak and bubble.

"That's the hole from the shot they shot at me," say Cue. "The blood most nearly dried, but it make me lame. But Israel's children, they's safe."

"They's across the river?" say the old woman.

"They's across the river," say Cue. "They ain't room for no more in the boat. But Sukey, she's across."

"And what will you do now, Son Cue?" say the old woman. "For that was your chance and your time, and you give it up for another. And tomorrow morning Mr. Wade, he'll see that hole in your leg and he'll ask questions. It's a heavy burden you've laid on yourself, Son Cue."

"It's a heavy burden," say Cue, "and I wish I was shut of it. I never asked to take no such burden. But freedom's a hard-bought thing."

The old woman stand up sudden, and for once she look straight and tall. "Now bless the Lord!" she say. "Bless the Lord and praise him! I come with my mammy in the slavery ship; I come with the middle passage. There ain't many that remember that, these days, or care about it. There ain't many that remember the red flag that witched us on board or how we used to be free. Many thousands gone, and the thousands of many thousands that lived and died in slavery. But I remember. I remember them all. Then they took me into the Big House—me that was a Mandingo and a witch woman—and the way I live in the Big House, that's between me and my Lord. If I done wrong, I done paid for it. I paid for it with weeping and sorrow. That's before Old Miss's time and I help raise up Old Miss. They sell my daughter to the South and my son to the West, but I raise up Old Miss and tend on her. I ain't going to repine of that. I count the hairs on Old Miss's head when she's young, and she turn to me, weak and helpless. And for that there'll be a kindness between me and the Big House, a kindness that folks will remember. But my children's children shall be free."

"You do this to me," say Cue, and he look at her and he look dangerous. "You do this to me, old woman," he say, and his breath come harsh in his throat, and his hands twitch.

"Yes," she say, and look him straight in the eyes. "I do to you what I never even do for my own. I do it for your granddaddy Shango, that never turn to me in the light of the fire. He turn to that soft Eboe woman, and I have to see it. He roar like a lion in the chains, and I have to see that. So, when you come, I try you and I test you, to see if you fit to follow after him. And because you fit to follow after him, I put freedom in your heart, Son Cue."

"I never going to be free," say Cue, and look at his hands. "I done broke all the rules. They bound to sell me now."

"You'll be sold and sold again," say the old woman. "You'll know the chains and the whip. I can't help that. You'll suffer for your people and with your people. But while one man's got freedom in his heart, his children bound to know the tale."

She put the lid on the pot and it stop bubbling. "Now I come to the end of my road," she say, "but the tale don't stop there. The tale go backward to Africa and it go forward, like clouds and fire. It go, laughing and grieving forever, through the earth and the air and the waters—my people's tale."

Then she drop her hands in her lap and Cue creep out of

the cabin. He know then he's bound to be a witness, and it make him feel cold and hot. He know then he's bound to be a witness and tell that tale. O Lord, it's hard to be a witness, and Cue know that. But it help him in the days to come.

Now, when he get sold, that's when Cue feel the iron in his heart. Before that, and all his life, he despise bad servants and bad marsters. He live where the marster's good; he don't take much mind of other places. He's a slave, but he's Cue, the blacksmith, and Old Marster and Old Miss, they tend to him. Now he know the iron in his heart and what it's like to be a slave.

He know that on the rice fields in the hot sun. He know that, working all day for a handful of corn. He know the bad marsters and the cruel overseers. He know the bite of the whip and the gall of the iron on the ankle. Yes, Lord, he know tribulation. He know his own tribulation and the tribulation of his people. But all the time, somehow, he keep freedom in his heart. Freedom mighty hard to root out when it's in the heart.

He don't know the day or the year, and he forget, half the time, there ever was a gal named Sukey. All he don't forget is the noise of the train in his ears, the train snorting and sparking underground. He think about it at nights till he dream it carry him away. Then he wake up with the horn. He feel ready to die then, but he don't die. He live through the whip and the chain; he live through the iron and the fire. And finally he get away.

When he get away he ain't like the Cue he used to be, not even back at Old Marster's place. He hide in the woods like a rabbit; he slip through the night like an owl. He go

cold and hungry, but the star keep shining over him and
he keep his eyes on the star. They set the dogs after him,
and he hear the dogs belling and yipping through the woods.

He's scared when he hear the dogs, but he ain't scared
like he used to be. He ain't more scared than any man. He
kill the big dog in the clearing—the big dog with the big
voice—and he do it with his naked hands. He cross water
three times after that to kill the scent, and he go on.

He got nothing to help him, no, Lord, but he got a star.
The star shine in the sky and the star shine—the star point
north with its shining. You put that star in the sky, O Lord;
you put it for the prisoned and the humble. You put it there;
you ain't never going to blink it out.

He hungry and he eat green corn and cowpeas. He thirsty
and he drink swamp water. One time he lie two days in the
swamp, too puny to get up on his feet, and he know they
hunting around him. He think that's the end of Cue. But
after two days he lift his head and his hand. He kill a
snake with a stone, and after he's cut out the poison bag,
he eat the snake to strengthen him and go on.

He don't know what the day is when he come to the
wide, cold river. The river yellow and foaming, and Cue
can't swim. But he hide like a crawdad on the bank; he
make himself a little raft with two logs. He know this
time's the last time and he's obliged to drown. But he put
out on the raft, and it drift him to the freedom side. He
mighty weak by then.

He mighty weak, but he careful. He know tales of Billy
Shea, the slave catcher; he remember those tales. He slide
into the town by night, like a shadow, like a ghost. He beg
broken victuals at a door; the woman give them to him, but

she look at him suspicious. He make up a tale to tell her, but he don't think she believe the tale. In the gutter he find a newspaper; he pick it up and look at the notices. There's a notice about a runaway man named Cue. He look at it and it make the heart beat in his breast.

He patient; he mighty careful. He leave that town behind. He got the name of another town, Cincinnati, and a man's name in that town. He don't know where it is; he have to ask his way, but he do it mighty careful. One man's face. He remember Aunt Rachel; he tell the yellow man he conjure his liver out if the yellow man tell him wrong. Then the yellow man scared and tell him right. He don't hurt the yellow man; he don't blame him for not wanting trouble. But he make the yellow man change pants with him, because his pants mighty ragged.

He patient; he very careful. When he get to the place he been told about he look all about that place. It's a big house; it don't look right. He creep around to the back, he creep and he crawl. He look in a window; he see white folks eating their supper. They just look like any white folks. He expect them to look different. He feel mighty bad. All the same, he rap at the window the way he been told. They don't nobody pay attention, and he just about to go away. Then the white man get up from the table and open the back door a crack. Cue breathe in the darkness.

"God bless the stranger the Lord sends us," say the white man in a low, clear voice, and Cue run to him and stumble, and the white man catch him. He look up and it's a white man, but he ain't like thunder and lightning.

He take Cue and wash his wounds and bind them up. He feed him and hide him under the floor of the house. He ask him his name and where he's from. Then he send him on. O Lord, remember thy tried servant, Asaph Brown! Remember his name!

They send him from there in a wagon, and he's hidden in the straw at the bottom. They send him from the next place in a closed cart with six others, and they can't say a word all night. One time a toll keeper ask them what's in the wagon, and the driver say, "Southern calico," and the toll keeper laugh. Cue always recollect that.

One time they get to big water, so big it look like the ocean. They cross that water in a boat; they get to the other side. When they get to the other side they sing and pray, and white folks look on, curious. But Cue don't even feel happy; he just feel he want to sleep.

He sleep like he never sleep before, not for days and years. When he wake up he wonder; he hardly recollect where he is. He lying in the loft of a barn. Ain't nobody around him. He get up and go out in the air. It's a fine sunny day.

He get up and go out. He say to himself, "I'm free, but it don't take hold yet." He say to himself, "This is Canada, and I'm free," but it don't take hold. Then he start to walk down the street.

The first white man he meet on the street, he scrunch up in himself and start to run across the street. But the white man don't pay him no mind. Then he know.

He say to himself in his mind, "I'm free. My name's Cue— John H. Cue. I got a strong back and strong arms. I got freedom in my heart. I got a first name and a last name and a middle name. I never had them all before."

He say to himself, "My name's Cue, John H. Cue. I got a name and a tale to tell. I got a hammer to swing. I got a tale to tell my people. I got recollection. I call my first son 'John Freedom Cue.' I call my first daughter, 'Come-Out-of-the Lion's-Mouth.' "

Then he walk down the street, and he pass a blacksmith shop. The blacksmith, he's an old man and he lift the hammer heavy. Cue look in that shop and smile.

He pass on; he go his way. And soon enough he see a girl like a peach tree—a girl named Sukey—walking free down the street.

A Diamond Guitar

TRUMAN CAPOTE

The nearest town to the prison farm is twenty miles away.
Many forests of pine trees stand between the farm and the
town, and it is in these forests that the convicts work; they
tap for turpentine. The prison itself is in a forest. You will
find it there at the end of a red, rutted road, barbed wire
sprawling like a vine over the walls. Inside, there live one
hundred and nine white men, ninety-seven Negroes, and
one Chinese. There are two sleep houses, great green wooden
buildings with tar-paper roofs. The white men occupy one,
the Negroes and the Chinese the other. In each sleep house
there is one large potbellied stove, but the winters are cold

here, and at night with the pines waving frostily and a freezing light falling from the moon, the men, stretched on their iron cots, lie awake with the fire colors of the stove playing in their eyes.

The men whose cots are nearest the stove are the important men, those who are looked up to or feared. Mr. Schaeffer is one of these. Mr. Schaeffer—for that is what he is called, a mark of special respect—is a lanky, pulled-out man. He has reddish, silvering hair, and his face is attenuated, religious; there is no flesh to him; you can see the workings of his bones, and his eyes are a poor, dull color. He can read and he can write; he can add a column of figures. When another man receives a letter, he brings it to Mr. Schaeffer. Most of these letters are sad and complaining. Very often Mr. Schaeffer improvises more cheerful messages and does not read what is written on the page. In the sleep house there are two other men who can read. Even so, one of them brings his letters to Mr. Schaeffer, who obliges by never reading the truth. Mr. Schaeffer himself does not receive mail, not even at Christmas. He seems to have no friends beyond the prison, and actually he has none there, that is, no particular friend. This was not always true.

One winter Sunday some winters ago Mr. Schaeffer was sitting on the steps of the sleep house carving a doll. He is quite talented at this. His dolls are carved in separate sections, then put together with bits of spring wire; the arms and legs move, the head rolls. When he has finished a dozen or so of these dolls, the captain of the farm takes them into town, and there they are sold in a general store. In this way Mr. Schaeffer earns money for candy and tobacco.

That Sunday, as he sat cutting out the fingers for a little

hand, a truck pulled into the prison yard. A young boy, handcuffed to the captain of the farm, climbed out of the truck and stood blinking at the ghostly winter sun. Mr. Schaeffer only glanced at him. He was then a man of fifty, and seventeen of those years he'd lived at the farm. The arrival of a new prisoner could not arouse him. Sunday is a free day at the farm, and other men who were moping around the yard crowded down to the truck. Afterward, Pick Axe and Goober stopped by to speak with Mr. Schaeffer.

Pick Axe said, "He's a foreigner, the new one is. From Cuba. But with yellow hair."

"A knifer, Cap'n says," said Goober, who was a knifer himself. "Cut up a sailor in Mobile."

"Two sailors," said Pick Axe. "But just a café fight. He didn't hurt them boys none."

"To cut off a man's ear? You call that not hurtin' him. They give him two years, Cap'n says."

Pick Axe said, "He's got a guitar with jewels all over it."

It was getting too dark to work. Mr. Schaeffer fitted the pieces of his doll together and, holding its little hands, set it on his knees. He rolled a cigarette. The pines were blue in the sundown light, and the smoke from his cigarette lingered in the cold, darkening air. He could see the captain coming across the yard. The new prisoner, a blond young boy, lagged a pace behind. He was carrying a guitar studded with glass diamonds that cast a starry twinkle, and his new uniform was too big for him. It looked like a Halloween suit.

"Somebody for you, Schaeffer," said the captain, pausing on the steps of the sleep house. The captain was not a hard man. Occasionally he invited Mr. Schaeffer into his office, and they would talk together about things they had read in the newspaper. "Tico Feo," he said, as though it were the name of a bird or a song, "this is Mr. Schaeffer. Do like him, and you'll do right."

Mr. Schaeffer glanced up at the boy and smiled. He smiled at him longer than he meant to, for the boy had eyes like strips of sky—blue as the winter evening—and his hair was as gold as the captain's teeth. He had a fun-loving face, nimble, clever. Looking at him, Mr. Schaeffer thought of holidays and good times.

"Is like my baby sister," said Tico Feo, touching Mr. Schaeffer's doll. His voice with its Cuban accent was soft and sweet as a banana. "She sit on my knee also."

Mr. Schaeffer was suddenly shy. Bowing to the captain, he walked off into the shadows of the yard. He stood there whispering the names of the evening stars as they opened in flower above him. The stars were his pleasure, but tonight they did not comfort him; they did not make him remember that what happens to us on earth is lost in the endless shine of eternity. Gazing at them—the stars—he thought of the jeweled guitar and its worldly glitter.

It could be said of Mr. Schaeffer that in his life he'd done only one really bad thing: he'd killed a man. The circumstances of that deed are unimportant, except to say that the man deserved to die and that for it Mr. Schaeffer was sentenced to ninety-nine years and a day. For a long while, for many years, in fact, he had not thought of how it was before he came to the farm. His memory of those times was like a house where no one lives and where the furniture has rotted away. But tonight it was as if lamps had been lighted through all the gloomy dead rooms. It had begun to happen when he saw Tico Feo coming through the dusk with his splendid guitar. Until that moment he had not been lonesome. Now, recognizing his loneliness, he felt alive. He had not wanted to be alive. To be alive was to remember brown rivers where the fish run, and sunlight on a lady's hair.

Mr. Schaeffer hung his head. The glare of the stars had made his eyes water.

The sleep house usually is a glum place, stale with the smell of men and stark in the light of two unshaded electric bulbs. But with the advent of Tico Feo it was as though a tropic occurrence had happened in the cold room, for when Mr. Schaeffer returned from his observance of the stars he came upon a savage and garish scene. Sitting cross-legged on a cot, Tico Feo was picking at his guitar with long swaying fingers and singing a song that sounded as jolly as jingling coins. Though the song was in Spanish, some of the men tried to sing it with him, and Pick Axe and Goober were dancing together. Charlie and Wink were dancing too, but separately. It was nice to hear the men laughing, and when Tico Feo finally put aside his guitar, Mr. Schaeffer was among those who congratulated him.

"You deserve such a fine guitar," he said.

"Is diamond guitar," said Tico Feo, drawing his hand over the vaudeville dazzle. "Once I have a one with rubies. But that one is stole. In Havana my sister work in a, how you say, where make guitar; is how I have this one."

Mr. Schaeffer asked him if he had many sisters, and Tico Feo, grinning, held up four fingers. Then, his blue eyes narrowing greedily, he said, "Please, mister, you give me a doll for my two little sister?"

The next evening Mr. Schaeffer brought him the dolls. After that he was Tico Feo's best friend, and they were always together. At all times they considered each other.

Tico Feo was eighteen years old and for two years had worked on a freighter in the Caribbean. As a child he'd gone to school with nuns, and he wore a gold crucifix around his neck. He had a rosary too. The rosary he kept wrapped in a green silk scarf that also held three other treasures: a bottle of Evening in Paris cologne, a pocket mirror, and a Rand Mc-Nally map of the world. These and the guitar were his only possessions, and he would not allow anyone to touch them. Perhaps he prized his map the most. At night, before the lights were turned off, he would shake out his map and show Mr. Schaeffer the places he'd been—Galveston, Miami, New Orleans, Mobile, Cuba, Haiti, Jamaica, Puerto Rico, the Virgin Islands—and the places he wanted to go to. He wanted to go almost everywhere, especially Madrid, especially the North Pole. This both charmed and frightened Mr. Schaeffer. It hurt him to think of Tico Feo on the seas and in far places. He sometimes looked defensively at his friend and thought, You are just a lazy dreamer.

It is true that Tico Feo was a lazy fellow. After that first evening he had to be urged even to play his guitar. At daybreak when the guard came to rouse the men, which he did by banging a hammer on the stove, Tico Feo would whimper like a child. Sometimes he pretended to be ill, moaned and rubbed his stomach; but he never got away with this, for the captain would send him out to work with the rest of the men. He and Mr. Schaeffer were put together on a highway gang. It was hard work, digging at frozen clay and carrying croker sacks filled with broken stone. The guard had always to be shouting at Tico Feo, for he spent most of the time trying to lean on things.

Each noon, when the dinner buckets were passed around, the two friends sat together. There were some good things in Mr. Schaeffer's bucket, as he could afford apples and candy bars from the town. He liked giving these things to his friend, for his friend enjoyed them so much, and he thought, You are growing; it will be a long time until you are a grown man.

Not all the men liked Tico Feo. Because they were jealous, or for more subtle reasons, some of them told ugly stories about him. Tico Feo himself seemed unaware of this. When the men gathered around him, and he played his guitar and sang his songs, you could see that he felt he was loved. Most of the men did feel a love for him; they waited for and depended upon the hour between supper and lights out. "Tico, play your box," they would say. They did not notice that afterward there was a deeper sadness than there had ever been. Sleep jumped beyond them like a jackrabbit, and their eyes lingered ponderingly on the firelight that creaked behind the grating of the stove. Mr. Schaeffer was the only one who understood their troubled feeling, for he felt it too. It was that his friend had revived the brown rivers where the fish run and the ladies with sunlight in their hair.

Soon Tico Feo was allowed the honor of having a bed near the stove and next to Mr. Schaeffer. Mr. Schaeffer had always known that his friend was a terrible liar. He did not listen for the truth in Tico Feo's tales of adventure, of conquests and encounters with famous people. Rather he took pleasure

in them as plain stories, such as you would read in a magazine, and it warmed him to hear his friend's tropic voice
whispering in the dark.

It was late January. The friends were sitting on the steps
of the sleep house, each with a cigarette in his hand. A moon
thin and yellow as a piece of lemon rind curved above them,
and under its light, threads of ground frost glistened like
silver snail trails. For many days Tico Feo had been drawn
into himself, silent as a robber waiting in the shadows. It was
no good to say to him, "Tico, play your box." He would only
look at you with smooth, under-ether eyes.

"Tell a story," said Mr. Schaeffer, who felt nervous and
helpless when he could not reach his friend. "Tell about
when you went to the racetrack in Miami."

"I not ever go to no racetrack," said Tico Feo, thereby ad-
mitting to his wildest lie, one involving hundreds of dollars
and a meeting with Bing Crosby. He did not seem to care. He
produced a comb and pulled it sulkily through his hair. A few
days before this comb had been the cause of a fierce quarrel.
One of the men, Wink, claimed that Tico Feo had stolen the
comb from him, to which the accused replied by spitting in
his face. They had wrestled around until Mr. Schaeffer and
another man got them separated. "Is my comb. You tell him!"
Tico Feo had demanded of Mr. Schaeffer. But Mr. Schaeffer
with a quiet firmness had said no, it was not his friend's
comb, an answer that seemed to defeat all concerned.

"Aw," said Wink, "if he wants it so much, let him keep
it."

And later, in a puzzled, uncertain voice, Tico Feo had said,
"I thought you was my friend."

I am, Mr. Schaeffer had thought, though he said nothing.

"I not go to no racetrack, and what I said about the widow woman, that is not true also." He puffed up his cigarette to a furious glow and looked at Mr. Schaeffer with a speculating expression. "Say, you have money, mister?"

"Maybe twenty dollars," said Mr. Schaeffer hesitantly, afraid of where this was leading.

"Not so good, twenty dollar," Tico said, but without disappointment. "No important, we work our way. In Mobile I have my friend Frederico. He will put us on a boat. There will not be trouble," and it was as though he were saying that the weather had turned colder.

There was a squeezing in Mr. Schaeffer's heart; he could not speak.

"Nobody here can run to catch Tico. He run the fastest."

"Shotguns run faster," said Mr. Schaeffer in a voice hardly alive. "I'm too old," he said, with the knowledge of age churning like nausea inside him.

Tico Feo was not listening. "Then, the world. The world, *el mundo,* my friend." Standing up, he quivered like a young horse. Everything seemed to draw close to him—the moon, the callings of screech owls. His breath came quickly and turned to smoke in the air. "Should we go to Madrid? Maybe someone teach me to bullfight. You think so, mister?"

Mr. Schaeffer was not listening either. "I'm too old," he said. "I'm too damned old."

For the next several weeks Tico Feo kept after him—the world, *el mundo,* my friend—and he wanted to hide. He would shut himself in the toilet and hold his head. Nevertheless, he was excited, tantalized. What if it could come true, the race with Tico across the forests and to the sea? And he imagined himself on a boat, he who had never seen the sea, whose whole life had been land rooted. During this time one of the convicts died, and in the yard you could hear the coffin being made. As each nail thudded into place, Mr. Schaeffer thought, This is for me; it is mine.

Tico Feo himself was never in better spirits; he sauntered about with a dancer's snappy, gigolo grace and had a joke for everyone. In the sleep house after supper his fingers popped at the guitar like firecrackers. He taught the men to cry *olé,* and some of them sailed their caps through the air.

When work on the road was finished, Mr. Schaeffer and Tico Feo were moved back into the forests. On Valentine's Day they ate their lunch under a pine tree. Mr. Schaeffer had ordered a dozen oranges from the town, and he peeled them slowly, the skins unraveling in a spiral; the juicier slices he gave to his friend, who was proud of how far he could spit the seeds—a good ten feet.

It was a cold, beautiful day, scraps of sunlight blew about them like butterflies, and Mr. Schaeffer, who liked working with the trees, felt dim and happy. Then Tico Feo said, "That one, he no could catch a fly in his mouth." He meant Armstrong, a hog-jowled man sitting with a shotgun propped between his legs. He was the youngest of the guards and new at the farm.

"I don't know," said Mr. Schaeffer. He'd watched Armstrong and noticed that, like many people who are both heavy and vain, the new guard moved with a skimming lightness. "He might could fool you."

"I fool him maybe," said Tico Feo, and spit an orange seed in Armstrong's direction. The guard scowled at him, then blew a whistle. It was the signal for work to begin. Sometime during the afternoon the two friends came together again; that is, they were nailing turpentine buckets onto trees that stood next to each other. At a distance below them a shallow bouncing creek branched through the woods. "In water no smell," said Tico Feo meticulously, as though remembering something he'd heard. "We run in the water until dark; then we climb a tree. Yes, mister?"

Mr. Schaeffer went on hammering, but his hand was shaking and the hammer came down on his thumb. He looked around dazedly at his friend. His face showed no reflection of pain, and he did not put the thumb in his mouth, the way a man ordinarily might.

Tico Feo's blue eyes seemed to swell like bubbles, and when in a voice quieter than the wind sounds in the pine tops he said, "Tomorrow," these eyes were all that Mr. Schaeffer could see.

"Tomorrow, mister?"

"Tomorrow," said Mr. Schaeffer.

The first colors of morning fell upon the walls of the sleep house, and Mr. Schaeffer, who had rested little, knew that Tico Feo was awake too. With the weary eyes of a crocodile he observed the movements of his friend in the next cot. Tico Feo was unknotting the scarf that contained his treasures. First he took the pocket mirror. Its jellyfish light trembled on his face. For a while he admired himself with serious delight, and combed and slicked his hair as though he were preparing to step out to a party. Then he hung the rosary about his neck. The cologne he never opened, nor the map. The last thing he did was to tune his guitar. While the other men were dressing, he sat on the edge of his cot and tuned the guitar. It was strange, for he must have known he would never play it again.

Bird shrills followed the men through the smoky morning woods. They walked single file, fifteen men to a group, and a guard bringing up the rear of each line. Mr. Schaeffer was sweating as though it were a hot day, and he could not keep in marching step with his friend, who walked ahead, snapping his fingers and whistling at the birds.

A signal had been set. Tico Feo was to call, "Time out," and pretend to go behind a tree. But Mr. Schaeffer did not know when it would happen.

The guard named Armstrong blew a whistle, and his men dropped from the line and separated to their various stations. Mr. Schaeffer, though going about his work as best he could, took care always to be in a position where he could keep an eye on both Tico Feo and the guard. Armstrong sat on a stump, a chew of tobacco lopsiding his face, and his gun pointing into the sun. He had the tricky eyes of a cardsharp; you could not really tell where he was looking.

Once another man gave the signal. Although Mr. Shaeffer had known at once that it was not the voice of his friend, panic had pulled at his throat like a rope. As the morning wore on there was such a drumming in his ears he was afraid he would not hear the signal when it came.

The sun climbed to the center of the sky. He is just a lazy dreamer. It will never happen, thought Mr. Schaeffer, daring a moment to believe this. But, "First we eat," said Tico Feo with a practical air as they set their dinner pails on the bank above the creek. They ate in silence, almost as though each bore the other a grudge, but at the end of it Mr. Schaeffer felt his friend's hand close over his own and hold it with a tender pressure.

"Mister Armstrong, time out. . . ."

Near the creek Mr. Schaeffer had seen a sweet gum tree, and he was thinking it would soon be spring and the sweet gum ready to chew. A razory stone ripped open the palm of his hand as he slid off the slippery embankment into the water. He straightened up and began to run. His legs were long, he kept almost abreast of Tico Feo, and icy geysers sprayed around them. Back and forth through the woods the shouts of men boomed hollowly like voices in a cavern, and there were three shots, all high-flying, as though the guard were shooting at a cloud of geese.

Mr. Schaeffer did not see the log that lay across the creek. He thought he was still running, and his legs thrashed about him. It was as though he were a turtle stranded on its back.

While he struggled there, it seemed to him that the face of his friend, suspended above him, was part of the white winter sky, it was so distant, judging. It hung there but an instant, like a hummingbird, yet in that time he'd seen that Tico Feo had not wanted him to make it, had never thought he would, and he remembered once thinking that it would be a long time before his friend was a grown man. When they found him, he was still lying in the ankle-deep water as though it were a summer afternoon and he were idly floating on the stream.

Since then three winters have gone by, and each has been said to be the coldest, the longest. Two recent months of rain washed deeper ruts in the clay road leading to the farm, and it is harder than ever to get there, harder to leave. A pair of searchlights have been added to the walls, and they burn there through the night like the eyes of a giant owl. Otherwise, there have not been many changes. Mr. Schaeffer, for instance, looks much the same, except that there is a thicker

frost of white in his hair, and as the result of a broken ankle
he walks with a limp. It was the captain himself who said
that Mr. Schaeffer had broken his ankle attempting to capture
Tico Feo. There was even a picture of Mr. Schaeffer in the
newspaper, and under it this caption: *Tried to Prevent
Escape*. At the time he was deeply mortified, not because
he knew the other men were laughing, but because he thought
of Tico Feo seeing it. But he cut it out of the paper anyway
and keeps it in an envelope along with several clippings
pertaining to his friend; a spinster woman told the authorities
he'd entered her home and kissed her, twice he was reported
seen in the Mobile vicinity, finally it was believed that he
had left the country.

No one has ever disputed Mr. Schaeffer's claim to the
guitar. Several months ago a new prisoner was moved into
the sleep house. He was said to be a fine player, and Mr.
Schaeffer was persuaded to lend him the guitar. But all the
man's tunes came out sour, for it was as though Tico Feo,
tuning his guitar that last morning, had put a curse upon it.
Now it lies under Mr. Schaeffer's cot, where its glass
diamonds are turning yellow. In the night his hand sometimes searches it out, and his fingers drift across the strings:
then, the world.

The White Mustang

JACK SCHAEFER

Old Jake Hanlon sits on the edge of the mesa and looks out over miles of southwestern plain. Mile upon mile it runs to hazy horizon, broken only by the sharp upthrusts of the few tall, lonely rocky buttes that still resist the long, slow erosion of time. They rise like islands in the immensity of open space.

Old Jake Hanlon sits as still and quiet as a wrinkled lizard on a sun-warmed stone. He is weathered and withered to a thin, angular shape of brittle bones and remnants of stringy muscle. His hatchet face under his wide, floppy hat brim has been whittled by age to dry, leathery skin stretched taut over the bone structure beneath. He is something like a rocky

butte himself. Old Jake has left the town for good and has
come out here to the abandoned headquarters of the Triple
X, to the tumbledown adobe house and the roofless barn and
the empty, broken-rail corrals that dwindle toward erasure
into the land. He has come out here along the old, washed-
out road no longer scraped by the county, bouncing on the
front seat of a fine, powerful car beside Henry W. Harper,
grandson of Hardrock Harper, who founded the Triple X
a long lifetime ago.

There is water from the spring back of the crumbling
house, only a trickle now, but enough. There is food in cans
on the shelf in the one room whose ceiling still shuts out the
sky. Once every two weeks Henry W. Harper drives the car
along that parody of a road, bringing more food in cans. He
is a plumpish, middle-aged man, this Henry W. Harper, with
soft hands and manicured nails and a fine big house in town.
But he was once young Hank, who learned from old Jake
Hanlon how to sit a saddle as a man should. He will be
bouncing over that forgotten road, bringing food in cans as
long as there is need for it.

That will not be long now. Old Jake has come out here,
where some of his best years were spent in the satisfaction of
sweat and dust and hard work. He has come out here to die.
He is an old grizzly that knows its time has come and has
retreated deep into its range to meet death in dignity alone.

Old Jake Hanlon sits on the mesa edge and puffs slowly on
an old crusted-bowl pipe that fouls the air above it as the
smoke drifts upward.

Below him on the great expanse of plain, out of sightless
distance to the east, into sightless distance to the west, snaking

between the tall, lonely buttes, runs the new highway. It is a dual highway with wide median strip, modern as the day after tomorrow. Small it seems in the vastness of plain and from his height on the mesa edge. But it is big in meaning, in the conquering of the distances, in the linking of far busy cities. Along it, both ways, in unending, fluctuating progression, flows the traffic that is its reason for being. Cars and cars and more cars. Long, sleek, powerful cars and smaller compacts and still smaller foreign models. Cars with gas pedals to the floor, racing hot engines past the speed limit, taking businessmen to appointments that mean dollars, tourists to the next comfortable, air-conditioned motels marked for them on their maps. Buses, big and ungainly, ripping away rubber trying to keep to impossible schedules. Huge tractor-trailer trucks with diesel exhausts snorting fumes, hammering the pavement in their rush to reach the haven of distant warehouses.

"All of 'em in one big hurry," says old Jake. "Tryin' to get somewheres. Ain't they ever figured they was somewheres afore they started?"

Still and quiet as a lizard on a rock, he sits and watches. And now the pipe has gone out, and he does not know that. He stares down at the flowing traffic, and he does not see it. His old eyes are brighter than before, and they look down on the big dual highway, but they do not see it. For him it has faded away into the mists of long ago, and there, where it snakes its way between the tall buttes, is only the thin tracery of an ancient trail. That murky veil hanging over the highway to the westward is not the gray, reeking smog from big trucks hammering the hard pavement. It is a rising cloud of clean, sweet dust, golden in glancing sunlight, raised by thousands of hooves drumming the good earth in the clean, sweet beat of freedom.

There they come, hooves thundering, manes flying, heads tossing, with the look of eagles in their eyes! The wild horses, the mustangs, the broncos, the broomtails.

Out of the West they come, in numbers past counting. Descendants of the gallant Barbs, with the blood of Arabia in them, brought from the plains of Córdoba in far-off Spain by the conquistadores four centuries ago. Home again in the land where the first horses evolved eons ago in the youth of the American continents and from there spread into Asia across the Alaskan land bridge before it sank and the ocean rolled between. Home again in the land where their remote ancestors came into being and then, in some cataclysmic shift of conditions as the years in their millennia swept past, dwindled into extinction. Home again in the land of their primal birth, the land that was ready to receive them again when they were brought from Spain and they escaped to run free once more.

Smallish and thin and bony, stunted through the years and by the generations of subsistence on the scant but hardy forage of the semiarid Southwest. Much of the Barb beauty is gone, the noble head, the arched neck, the straight back, the full-fleshed, swelling hips. Smallish and stunted, grass-bellied, cat-hipped. Almost everything splendid gone—everything except the spirit and the hardihood. And the stubborn clutch on freedom. Bred by adversity to a single purpose, survival in a land where only those fitted to it can survive.

Out of the West they come, herd by herd in their groupings past counting, wise old barren mares in the lead, with the younger following with foals by their sides, and the lordly studs behind, stern stallions herding their harems, nipping the stragglers, shouldering the laggards, all the wild ones old Jake Hanlon has seen through the misty long ago, when he was a boy on the seat of a wagon moving into the setting sun and when he was a hard-riding mustanger with the best of them and when he was a reckless, carefree cowhand riding the farthest ranges.

They flow past, traffic out of another era, and old Jake nods his head as he recognizes this one and that one passing his lonely post on the high mesa. On beyond, faint in the distance, is a flush of green in a dip of the plain that marks a water hole, and one of the bands swings toward it. Old Jake is quiet on the mesa edge, yet he is no longer there. He is out near the water hole, crawling on hands and knees through the bunchgrass. And now he is a thick-shanked boy in torn shirt and patched pants too big for him, and he is lying on the top of the slight rise swelling around the water hole, flat on his belly, peering over.

There they come, off to his left, topping the rise. They stop, and the stud trots forward, a battle-scarred dun in the full pride of power and lordship. He stands with head high, testing the wind, looking in every direction. He whistles softly, and the band moves forward, downslope, to the water hole.

All but one, a mare, thin and gaunt, lagging behind. The others have left her, hurrying on down. She moves slowly and stiffly, as if afraid of each forward step. Something is wrong with her, something serious. She steps forward and brushes against an upthrust cactus and flinches back and stands shuddering. Blind in both eyes.

The others are dipping muzzles, crowding one another for

position. No, not the stud. He has trotted back up the slope toward the blind mare. He nudges her to one side, away from the cactus. He nickers softly, coaxing her into motion, and she follows him, nose against his warm, comforting, battle-scarred flank. She hesitates, feeling the downslope under her feet, and he snorts a command and she follows. His great shoulders open a way through the others, and she pushes in behind him and dips her muzzle and drinks.

The stud drinks only in brief dippings, raising his head often to test the wind. Suddenly he whistles, loud and shrill. He has caught the man scent in a shift of breeze. Instantly the whole band wheels away from the water and leaps into motion, following the wise old lead mare. The blind mare wheels too and strikes out, seeking to follow, but slow and hesitant. The stud is on her, pushing, nipping, shouldering, driving her into full gallop. She stretches out, shoulder to shoulder with him, and he has her up with the others. He drives her in among them, and she gallops on unhesitating now, swerving as they swerve, with the sound and the sense and the smell and the feel of them all about her. He stops and swings about, looking back. He trumpets defiance at whatever might follow and rears high, wheeling, and races after his harem.

"Nobody won't believe me anymore," says old Jake Hanlon. "But I seen it. I sure seen it."

All of them are gone now, all the bands, from out of the West into the nothingness of time past. They are no longer flowing by even in the mind of old Jake Hanlon. Once again the ancient trail is a big, new, modern dual highway with mechanical power pouring along it. But wait. Old Jake is not looking at the highway, is not even aware of it. He is

looking over it, beyond it, into the dimming distance. That is
not a dust devil whirling upward that he sees on the far
horizon. It is a cloud of golden dust rising from pounding
hooves!

This is the famous one, alone, all alone in the vastness of
space, glowing in the glancing sunlight, white, white as the
snow of the tall desert mountains in winter, with head high
and long mane flying and longer tail streaming in the wind
of his matchless motion, pacing, pacing, pacing in long,
swinging, unbroken strides! The white mustang, the white
steed of the prairies, the ghost horse of the plains.

Not a part of the whole wild West that has not known him.
If not this one, then another, and all always the same. The
final absolute of the wild, free life. The king of the broncos.
The king dies, and still it is long live the king! Always he is
sighted again somewhere across the far ranges of the American West. He is indomitable, unconquerable, and he cannot
ever really die because he is the stuff of which legends are
made, and he lives deep in the minds of men, the symbol of
their own stubborn clutch on freedom. Every man must have
his white mustang, his dream to follow, the glowing white
glimmer that paces ahead of his own plodding progress.
Lucky the man who sees it plain in the proud days of his
youth and can see it still undimmed on through the long
years of growing old.

Nearly three hundred miles this one has run this time,
with scarcely a stop or a breather. Four days and the nights
between and no food except a few mouthfuls of grass
snatched almost in stride. No water except a few swallows
scooped each time he has crossed the shallow, almost-dry
riverbed in the great sweeping seventy-mile circuits he has

been making of this range that has been his and that he will not leave. He is too wise to take on more water and be slowed in the running.

Those two dark dots coming into sight a third of a mile behind him are two men on horseback. They are erect in saddles on two fresh horses picked up only a few miles back. At fifteen-mile intervals around the great circuit other men wait with other fresh horses, wait for their turns in the long chase to push him, push him, push him and run him down at last.

Five thousand dollars pace with him. That is the sum the famous showman P. T. Barnum has offered for capture of this white mustang. A big sum to the men of the Southwest, big even if split many ways. Many of them have joined together to try to do what some of them have tried in vain to do before. Ten men and fifty horses are running the white mustang.

They have studied his habits and know his range. Four days they have been running him and the nights between, because through these moonlit nights the whiteness of him can be followed as in the daytime. The yearling colts and the mares of his band have long since dropped away, exhausted and left behind. Still he paces on. Again and again rested men on rested horses, starting from stations along the circuit, have tried to close in on him with ropes ready. Always the rhythmic beat of those four rock-hard hooves has quickened and the swinging stride has lengthened and he has pulled away to a safe lead once more.

Old Jake Hanlon sits on the mesa edge. He is still and quiet, but memories move in his withered old muscles. Strange, it is not stone nor sand nor clean adobe dirt beneath his lean old buttocks. It is good leather with the sweat of miles soaked into it. He is motionless as a rooted tree, yet he can feel the wind of movement fanning the dry skin of his face. He is no longer there on the mesa. He is one of those distant dots far out on the limitless plain. He is tall in the saddle on a rough-built, rawboned sorrel he has broken to the bit himself. He is young Jake Hanlon, top-hand rider of the rough string for the Triple X, and he is running the white mustang.

They hammered on, side by side in the afternoon sun, young Jake Hanlon and Petey Corle, following the white glimmer of the ghost horse. They were grim, determined, not joshing each other as they had been only the day before. The long strain was telling on them despite the periods of rest while others took up the running. They were no longer merely following him to keep him moving with no rest and little or no food and water. They were pushing him harder now, trying to close in more often. The long strain was telling on him, too. Nothing made of muscle and bone could keep on forever in that endless, tiring circuit. Yes, it was telling on him. That showed in the way he let them draw closer each time and in the gradually diminishing lead he established in each new spurt.

Young Jake felt a slow, rising eagerness. He rode with eyes fixed on the white glimmer always ahead. He thought he saw a falter in the swinging stride, and the eagerness swept through him. He knew the mettle of the horse under him, the power and speed in the rawboned frame that could show heels to any other horse broken to saddle in the whole of the country around. He slapped spurs, and the sorrel surged forward into full gallop.

Closer, closer. Young Jake could see the sweat streaks along the white flanks. He could hear the low, sobbing whistle as breath entered and left the laboring lungs. His rope was in his hands, and a loop was forming.

The head of the white mustang rose higher and turned some, and young Jake saw the red-rimmed eye that placed him and the sorrel coming up. He heard the snort of defiance that seemed to him to be touched with derision, too. The beat of those rock-hard hooves that had never known shoes quickened, quickened, drumming the earth, and the stride lengthened, and the white mustang was pulling away, faster, faster, leaving him far behind.

Young Jake slumped lower in the saddle. He could feel the sorrel striving under him, giving all that it had in its willing, rawboned frame. He reached to slap it gently along the straining neck. "You might as well be tied to a post," he said. He slapped again, friendly, forgiving. "Don't take it rough," he said. "You carryin' weight, an' he ain't."

Young Jake tightened on reins to slow the pace and waited for Petey to catch up. Together they rode on, following, merely following.

Through the late afternoon and evening and on through the night with the waning moon rising late, ten men and fifty horses, taking their turns in pairs, followed that ghostly glimmer of whiteness on the great circuit of the range that he would not leave.

Young Jake Hanlon and Petey Corle, sleepless, hunched on heels by a small fire. They talked together, and young Jake saddled one of the horses picketed near and rode through the night to the next station back and talked to Ace Hogarty and Ansel Rak, and they nodded their heads at what he said, and he rode the return to Petey and their fire, and by the first light of morning all was ready.

There he came, out of the dawn, the dawn of the fifth day of the running, stride unbroken but head drooping at last, flecks of foam dropping from his muzzle along the way, pace lagging. Ace and Ansel behind him were not pushing hard. But they had been riding out to the right, crowding him more and more to the left along a ragged-edge row of hills. Now he was approaching the narrow entrance of a steep-walled canyon that cut back into those hills. In a moment more he would be past it.

Out from their hidden post in juniper and climbing scrub oak rode young Jake Hanlon and Petey Corle, cutting across his path from the right.

He braked on sliding hooves and wheeled to the left and in a desperate spurt started in through the canyon entrance.

Started. Stopped. He knew. He knew every mile and rod and yard and foot of this range. He knew that on ahead in the canyon was only steep-walled, cramped space ending in sheer-rising cliff. A natural corral. A trap. He turned and faced the rock-edged entrance and the two horsemen blocking it now with ropes ready in hands. He screamed once, high and shrill, defiance and the exaltation of battle in it, and drove forward.

Petey first, Petey Corle, firm in saddle on a stout young gray, proud of his skill with a rope, spurring in to have first chance. There was no chance. Straight as a bullet leaving a gun, unswerving, the white mustang crashed into the gray, shoulder to shoulder in shuddering impact, and the gray staggered and went down, and Petey was rolling on the ground with the rope trailing from numbed fingers.

Young Jake next. Young Jake Hanlon, deep set in double-cinched saddle on a big-muscled dun, proud of his record in the taking of mustangs. He had swung the dun broadside to close off as much as possible of the canyon opening. His loop was ready for the cast as the ghost horse would race past through the narrow space remaining. The white mustang did not race past. Straight toward young Jake he came, and he reared on hind legs, up, up in the terrifying stance of the fighting stallion.

Young Jake saw the sweat-stained, dirt-streaked chest arching upward only a few feet from him. He saw the fore-legs with their knife-sharp hooves rising for the downward flailing strokes. He saw the foam-flecked lips drawn back from the big teeth. He saw the look of eagles in the red-rimmed, bloodshot eyes. The rope was a forgotten thing in his hands. It fell from them, and he grabbed at the reins to swing the dun away, and the white mustang struck. One forehoof snapped young Jake's hat brim and raked down his side just back of the arm, slicing through leather vest and flannel shirt, drawing blood and cracking two ribs and knocking him from the saddle. The other cut a long gash in the neck of the dun. And even as he fell to hit the ground hard, young Jake heard the snap of the big teeth like the jaws of a bear trap closing as they hit and slid on the hide of the rump of the dun, as frantic in frenzy it leaped away.

Young Jake lay on the ground, lip bruised and bloody but with head raised, and watched the white mustang moving away in the distance, and Ace Hogarty and Ansel Rak coming up.

"So it didn't work," said Ansel with a wry, weary grin.

"It sure didn't," said young Jake. He sat up, wincing at the pain streaks in his side. He managed a wry, weary, answering grin. "But you two keep right on goin'," he said. "Keep him movin'. Petey and me, we'll patch each other up and gather the others for a finish. We got him now."

"Whammed you on the head," said Ace. "Plumb locoed. Five days. Us an' the hosses about wore out. An' he's still goin' strong."

"No," said young Jake "You ain't noticed? Must of been when he piled into Petey. He's limpin'."

On through the morning and into the afternoon the white mustang ran. But that matchless pace was ragged now, and he slowed often, looking back, and spurted on again only when those following were not much more than a double rope length behind. Along in the late afternoon he topped out on a high rise and looked back, and there were no horsemen following. There was only open plain rolling to the far hills and mountains of the horizon.

He stopped. For long moments he scanned the plain in every direction, head high, testing the wind. Nothing moved anywhere except a small herd of antelope several miles away. He stood, and slowly the heaving of his chest subsided. He stood, and the weariness held at bay during the tension of the running crept through him, and the muscles of his swollen shoulder tightened in a taut and painful stiffness.

Hunger gnawed in his belly, and he dropped his head to graze. Not for long. Thirst was a stronger command. Slowly, cautiously, limping, favoring the bruised shoulder, he worked his way downwind and in a wide arc toward a curving sweep of the riverbed. He came to a shallow pool under the shelving bank. He drank again.

Still there was no message along the wind, no movement

alien to his instinct. He was turning away, fully watered, when he heard the long-drawn whinny of a mare. One of his mares.

The sound came from across the riverbed, up and over the low, stony hill that sent the river in rain time on its sweep around. He stood motionless, head up, ears forward, listening. It came again, a long-drawn, lonesome appeal. Silently, hooves making no sound in the soft ground, he moved down-river to the left, along the bank. The limp was very noticeable now, the stiffened shoulder muscles rebelling at movement, but he disregarded that. He crossed the riverbed where low-land on both sides gave wide vision and moved on in an arc flanking the low hill. In the hollow behind it he saw her.

He whistled softly, and she turned and started toward him. And stopped, legs braced, head twisted at a strange angle. He whistled again, and she answered strangely, breath wheezing in her throat. Puzzled, he advanced toward her and, advancing, saw the rope tight about her neck and taut to the stake in the ground and, seeing, heard the sound of hooves to his right and, turning, saw the two horsemen pounding toward him. He wheeled again and was off again, angling away from the horsemen now dashing at full gallop to intercept him. Even so, heavy with water, lean and worn with the weariness of five days' running, agony striking upward into his shoulder with each stroke of hoof, he would have outrun them. But more horsemen appeared ahead of him, fanning out, and the circle was complete.

He did not hesitate or waste time in shifting direction, seeking to dodge. Reckless of the pain beating in his shoulder, he drove on in that matchless, power-drive pace. Big Jim

Hawkins, on a big long-coupled black, blocked the way, and at the last minute Jim spurred aside and big Jim's rope flashed and the loop dropped over the straining white head. He drove on. The rope tightened with a snap to big Jim's saddle horn, and the black was yanked off its feet and dragged, and big Jim floundered on the ground, with an ankle sprained and the skin of one cheek scraped off. The cinch broke and the white mustang drove on, with the saddle bouncing at the rope end behind him.

He was through the circle and away, but the saddle caught in a low, tough juniper, and he spun about, with the rope cutting deep into his neck. Instantly his big jaws closed on it and grated together in grinding motion, and the rope parted. Only a few seconds. But that was enough. Arnie Hall's rope was in the air and caught him as he whirled to start away again.

He knew what a rope meant now, and as it tightened on his neck, he did not fight it. Instead he plunged back along it toward Arnie, rearing to strike. But young Jake Hanlon was racing in close, and young Jake had a small loop reach, and this flipped and took one of the rising forelegs. As young Jake plowed on, the white mustang was pulled aside and off balance and crashed on his side to the ground.

Two ropes were on him, neck and foreleg, pulling in opposite directions. Still he heaved to his feet and fought, lunging from side to side, striking at the ropes with snapping jaws. But now Petey Corle was there, clever with a rope and with yesterday's failure to avenge. His loop flicked out low to the ground and had a hind leg, and the white mustang was down again.

He pitched and thrashed, but the ropes held, and he could not rise. He seemed to sense the futility of further fight and lay still.

Nine men in saddles and a tenth standing with weight mostly on one foot looked down at the ghost horse of the plains. Thin and gaunt he was from the long running, with hollowed flanks and the ribs showing under the hide. Sweated and dirtied he was, with the whiteness of him smudged into yellowish splotches and the luster of mane and tail lost back along the miles. Awkward he looked, with foreleg and hind one stretched out and neck pulled awry by the third rope. But they had seen him in motion and action. They knew they were looking at more horse than any of them had been that close to before through all the years of their lives.

"I ain't so sure," said big Jim Hawkins, holding his neckerchief to skinned, bloody cheek, "that if I'd a known what it took to take him, I'd of started out on this."

"He don't look like so much right now," said Ace Hogarty. "All the same, if any of you was to ask me, I'd say that old Barnum'll be gettin' his money's worth."

And nine men were talking, letting the excitement of the last few moments ease out of them in words. But young Jake Hanlon said nothing. He sat slumped in saddle, staring down at the white mustang he had followed through five days of riding and two cracked ribs. He saw the red-rimmed, blood-shot eyes that were fixed now far off into limitless space, ignoring him and the other men, looking past them, beyond them, into the dimming distance of the big land.

He shook himself a bit and straightened in saddle, wincing as the movement revived the pain streaks in his side. "Let's

get movin'," he said. "We ain't penned him yet. I ain't a-goin'
to be sure of my five hundred till we do."

It took till dusk to get him, front legs hobbled and three
ropes tight to his neck, to the small corral they had prepared
before the running. A stout corral with stockade-style walls
seven feet high. On his feet again he fought most of the way,
lunging often against the ropes until each time the cross pull
choked him into weakness, and his legs faltered and his
breath rattled and his eyes glazed. They threw him again
and hobbled his hind legs, too, before they let him struggle
up, and they pulled him inside. When he was in there alone,
with the high, strong gate fastened behind him, he looked
around at the stout walls. His head drooped, and he stood
motionless. There was hay in a corner, but he ignored it.
There was water in a pail, but he ignored that, too. Only once
while they watched in the deepening dusk did he move.
Along one side of the corral a twist in one of the upright logs
left a four-inch gap partway up between it and the one next
to it. He raised his head some and shifted position in the hops
that were all the hobbles permitted until he could see out
through the narrow opening. There he stood, motionless
again except for the slow rhythm of his chest, looking through
a four-inch gap into the distance of what had been his range
while darkness claimed it.

They had a fire going and food and coffee warming. In the
firelight after they had eaten, Ansel Rak took a pack of
greasy cards from a pocket and shuffled them, and they cut
the deck, one after another, and the two high men swung
into saddles and rode into the dark. Sometime the next
morning they would be back with a flatbed hay wagon. No

chances would be taken in getting the white mustang to the rail town forty miles away. He would go there, lashed to the wagon bed.

The darkness deepened, and then the late waning moon rose, tinting the big land with its thin, ghostly traces of half-light, and seven of the remaining men slept in sprawled shapes on the ground. Not young Jake Hanlon. He was as tired as the others, but he could not sleep. His side ached. It seemed impossible for him to find a comfortable position on the ground. He pushed up to a sitting position and stared at the dark shape of the corral. He rose to his feet and walked softly to the tall gate and stepped up on a crosspiece to peer over. The mustang stood where he had been.

"It ain't a-goin' to be so bad," said young Jake. "They'll feed you regular and fix you up fancy. Likely they'll not try breakin' you to more'n bein' led along in a parade. Might even give you some mares for breedin'. Easy livin', that's what it'll be."

Young Jake stepped back down from the gate and walked slowly back to his saddle blanket spread on the ground. He lowered himself onto it. "Easy livin'," he murmured. "Who wants easy livin'?" He lay still, staring upward, and slowly his eyes closed, and he slept the sleep of tired muscles.

As the red flush of dawn crept over the plain, it was Ansel Rak who first stretched long and slow and rose and strolled over to the gate and stepped up to look into the corral. His shouts woke the others. The great white ghost horse was gone.

There was nothing ghostly about it. White hairs and bloodstains on the top of the far side of the stockade walls showed where he had reared and put forelegs over and scraped and scrambled and floundered until he had fallen outside. The tracks led away, unmistakable in the soft earth, where he had crow-hopped in short leaps on hobbled hooves and fallen often and struggled up to hop on.

He could not have gone far, not so weakened and so handicapped. They saddled fast and strung out along the trail. Straight toward the riverbed it led. There they found him at the edge of a shallow pool of water and mud, body crumpled down, muzzle buried in the watery ooze.

"Drowned hisself," said Ansel Rak. "In two inches of water."

Eight men looked down at what remained of the white mustang, at the $5,000 lost to them; seven of them let feelings loose in curses and bitter comments. Not young Jake Hanlon. He sat tall in the saddle on a rough-built, raw-boned sorrel he had broken to bit himself, and his shoulders were up and his head was high and he rubbed one hand down his side, where aching twinges of remembrance bothered him some. He looked around somewhat defiantly at the others.

"I sure could of used my share of the money," he said. "But I'm kind of glad that one got away."

Rock River Fugitive

MARY ROBERTS RINEHART

"Right over there," said the conductor, pointing to a low line of hills that lay blue gray in the distance, "about fifteen miles back, fully a hundred men are closing in on Devil's Peak, where they think he's hiding. The sheriff has a party out, too, trying to get him back to jail alive. But they'll never get him."

"Why not?" asked the young man, who was standing beside him on the platform.

"Why? Well, just because some of these fool politicians in Bucks County have put in a new sheriff lately, and while I haven't anything against him, having never had any dealings with him, fellows that know say he's a tenderfoot who don't know the business end of a gun from the butt. Nice fellow for a sheriff!"

The young man stretched his arms and looked at his watch. "Well, I'd better be getting my things together," he said. "She's almost due."

"That reminds me," said the conductor, turning back in the doorway. "Tom Watson, the engineer in Number 11, says he's seen a fellow about the build of Owens skulking around Rock River ravine for a couple of days. He may be waiting to board a freight on the siding there, you know. You'd better look to your guns."

The train slackened speed and stopped. From the baggage car, piece by piece, were unceremoniously bundled the constituent parts of a portable camping outfit. The conductor signaled to the engineer, and a moment later the solitary passenger stood watching the rear platform of the train disappear around a curve.

There was no station house in sight, and aside from the single railroad track with its accompaniment of telegraph poles there was no sign of human occupation. Thickly wooded hills sloped steeply to the track, and in one place where the creek, dignified as Rock River, had swerved to one side a siding had found room to crawl, affording a temporary refuge for the very occasional freight trains that chose the Chestnut Burr route.

The late afternoon sun had already left the platform in shadow, and a chilly breath from down the valley warned the young man that he had many things to do before night set in. He unstrapped from his shoulder the specimen box which told the object of his visit and, throwing off his well-worn shooting coat, fell vigorously to work.

At the end of an hour he had set up a small shelter tent just back of the platform which constituted the station, and a brisk fire was burning in the sheet-iron camp stove, over which his tall figure might have been seen stooping solicitously. Before long the odor of fried bacon, that invariable accompaniment of the camp stove, was filling the narrow gully and rising odorously through the trees above.

Had there been any observers, it would have been apparent that the lonely camper was expecting a visitor, for at intervals during his work he straightened himself to look closely up and down the track. But his meal of bacon and coffee had been finished, and the diminutive frying pan, tin cup, and plate had been washed in the creek across the track, before a slouching figure emerged from the woods and approached the camp. The newcomer came down the ties, his keen, suspicious eyes taking in every detail before him—the small white tent, the red glow of the fire, and the camper, whittling a piece of firewood dreamily on the edge of the station platform.

The latter was seemingly oblivious of his approach, but as he came within speaking distance the whittler stopped to ask curtly, "Late, aren't you?"

The newcomer, startled, took his hand from his hip pocket. "Well, mebbe I am," he said, as if the matter had not occurred to him before in that light.

"If the kit hadn't been too much for one man, I'd have started without you, and been to White Rocks by now. As it is, we'll have to stay here tonight and start early in the morning. You know the country pretty well, I suppose?"

"I reckon I know every hollow tree and every hole in the ground around these parts," was the reply, with a grim humor that seemed lost on his companion.

"Mosby's your name, isn't it?"

"That's as good as any. What's yours?"

"My name was signed to the letter you received—Gates, J. W. Gates." Mr. Gates was looking slightly irritated. "You were recommended to me as the best guide in this part of the country, but you've made me lose a great deal of valuable time already."

"No offense, Mr. J. W. Gates." Mosby took off a dilapidated soft hat, creased the crown carefully, and replaced it at the proper angle. "It was the initials that put me off. Folks in this neighborhood as a rule ain't got any. Glad enough, most of 'em, to have a name."

"Got blankets?" asked Gates, tendering some chocolate as a truce. This guide seemed a man to conciliate.

Mosby ignored the question. He was feeling through his pockets and shaking his head dejectedly. "Must have lost my knife along with the rest," he said. "Went to sleep about noon down the creek a few miles, an' woke up with everything gone. I followed the trail through the woods a bit, an' that's what kep' me late. Every blame thing's gone."

If Gates's face did not express any great degree of credulity, he at least refrained from giving expression to his doubts. "I'm somewhat shy on blankets," he said, as he produced and offered another bar of chocolate, "but I guess we'll manage somehow."

The two men sat there in silence for a time. The short twilight faded into darkness, and the trees stood faintly black against the skyline. Once the chorus of the frogs and crickets was momentarily eclipsed as Number 11, the solitary evening train on the branch, rushed by, the heavy smoke from the engine reflecting swift flashes of light from the furnace beneath. As the lanterns on the rear platform of the train faded from view, Mosby rose and stretched.

"Turning-in time, I reckon." He yawned. "Kind o' chilly, too. If you're shy on blankets, I'll build a fire. We'll be better off than in that baby tent."

Gates assented, and they were soon rolled in their blankets by a brush fire, which had been supplemented by coal from the railroad. Mosby seemed extremely weary. In an incredibly short time he was breathing the heavy, long-drawn respiration of exhausted sleep. Gates lay very still, apparently sleeping. In reality his every nerve was quivering. For what seemed like hours he lay there, watching the bright blaze of the fire fade to a warm, subdued glow. Then quietly and cautiously he raised himself to his elbow, his eyes on the prostrate man near him. The heavy breathing continued, but just as Gates rose to his feet there was a swift movement from Mosby, and a flash. Something fell clattering to the ground, and Gates, swung partly around by the force of the blow, sat down suddenly, with a groan. A bullet had gone nearly through the palm of his right hand, and the wound was bleeding profusely. He felt awkwardly with his left hand for a handkerchief to stanch the blood, Mosby watching him with an unpleasant smile.

"I don't approve of handlin' weapons so keerless like, an' in the middle of the night, too. Sorry to spoil that nice white hand of yours, but you needn't let a little thing like that spoil your huntin' trip, or whatever it is."

He picked up Gates's revolver, pocketed it, and systematically searched its owner for its mate. That secured, he seated himself judicially on the edge of the station platform and proceeded to discuss the situation, while Gates, weak with loss of blood and helplessly raging, lay by the embers of the fire.

"Now," he said, fingering cheerfully the knife which he had extracted from the injured man's pocket, "things is somethin' like this. That hand won't be hurtin' so much in the morning an' while you won't be quite so handy with a gun there ain't nothin' I see to keep you from goin' on with your little trip. This here's a pretty good outfit, an' I ain't for wastin' it. I've been lookin' for a chance to get 'cross the range for some time, but some friends of mine been so blamed anxious to meet me an' keep me here that I ain't gettin' there very fast. What is it you're after?"

"Geological specimens—rocks," said Gates wearily.

"Well, here's my little scheme, and I think you'll find it convenient to agree. We'll strike 'cross the range toward the state line; you're huntin' rocks, an' I'm your guide. If we meet any folks you stick it out—an' mind, a wink to the other fellows, an' you'll get the first bullet in the scrap."

He pulled out with a flourish the gold watch he had taken from Gates and opened it, holding it up in the firelight. "Two hours yet to sunup. Say, who's your lady friend?"

On the inner side of the lid was fastened a small photograph of Gates's mother.

Gates ground his teeth savagely, but, realizing his disadvantage, lay quiet.

"Real nice-lookin' girl," went on his tormentor. This was more than the other man could stand. With a choking oath he leaped to his feet and struck Mosby full in the mouth with his clenched left hand. They grappled, but the odds were too great. Gates, in spite of his youth and college training, was weakened by loss of blood, and in a few moments he was prone on the ground, his antagonist's knee on his chest.

"I've a mighty good notion to put a hole through your other hand for that," said Mosby, wiping away the blood from his lip. "But I reckon you'll be more useful the way you are. We're goin' to break camp now, so get up here an' hustle round. Breakin' in on my sleep the way you done makes me feel bad, so I'll sit here and watch." Which he proceeded to do, a revolver on either knee, ready to shoot at the slightest provocation.

Gates had bandaged his hand, and now with infinite labor and discomfort he packed up the outfit. There was no escape. No train was due for fully two hours, and even had Mosby's vigilance relaxed for an instant he was too weak to run for any distance. He was far from despairing, however, having the sanguine temperament of self-reliant youth.

The packing finished, Mosby shouldered his share of the burden, and with the first rays of the dawn they were picking their way along the wagon trail which led back through the hills, Mosby in the rear, his revolver in his hand.

Not far from the railroad they left the trail and struck into the hills. For hours they climbed steep wooded slopes, now making their way where going was easy, through pine woods with their springy carpet of needles, and again forcing their painful progress through dense underbrush and thickets. The two men traveled in silence. When Gates flagged, as occasionally he did, Mosby would request him to move on in a tone which required no interpreter. Once they stopped and in the shade of some giant rocks made a light breakfast of canned meat and bread, washing it down with water in lieu of coffee. It was evident that Mosby feared to attract pursuit by building a fire. During the afternoon they got out of the foothills and into the range itself. They were following now a kind of rough trail, and, although the ascents were steep, the presence of a path made progress easier. Once, as the trail skirted a steep bluff, they saw far below the smoke of a fire and some grazing ponies. With an oath Mosby drew his companion back into the brush and pressed forward at a speed that was almost beyond Gates's endurance.

Night found them well into the mountains, and Mosby's vigilance relaxed somewhat. He lighted a fire, and they tasted the first hot food of the day. In spite of himself Gates made a grimace when he tasted the coffee. Mosby turned on him with a scowl.

"Better make it yourself if you're so all-fired hard to please," he said sourly, and relapsed into glum silence.

The night was uneventful. They slept with a fire and were abroad early. Gates made the coffee, and breakfast was eaten in silence. The trail became so involved that Mosby was compelled to lead the way, his prisoner following. Had Gates cherished any hope of escape the previous day, he must have abandoned it now, for rapid flight was out of the question. His hand was troubling him less, and he began to take more interest in his surroundings. It was then that he noticed the berries. They were a satiny, violet black, about the size of a cherry, and the bush which bore them raised its broad, downy leaves almost to a level with his elbow. Gates eyed the bush suspiciously and stopped long enough to slip one of the berries into his mouth. Its sweetish taste confirmed his belief, and he took good care not to swallow any of it. At the next bush of the kind that they passed, he contrived to slip into his pocket, unnoticed, a handful of the berries, with fervent prayer that they might be what he hoped.

They had made good progress during the day, and Mosby was inclined to be merry. They camped that night in a small clearing, with a noisy little mountain creek close by. Gates cooked the supper, while Mosby lounged and said nothing. The bacon supply being almost exhausted, the meal consisted of canned soup, sardines, and coffee, and into both soup and coffee Gates dropped some of the pulp from the berries. On the plea of intense pain in his hand, he ate nothing, but Mosby stopped in the midst of his meal, dropping his mask of friendliness.

"Here, you, eat something. Think I'm goin' to have you gettin' sick and weak on my hands, with fifty miles to cover yet? Either you eat enough to keep up, or I'll fill you so full of lead you can't travel." What might have happened had Mosby forced him, at the revolver's point, to eat, Gates never knew, for at that moment the other man dropped his tin cup to the ground and, rising slowly, took two or three dizzy steps forward. Then he stumbled and fell, his muscles twitching convulsively, his chest heaving laboriously for breath. His face from being deadly pale became scarlet, and the pupils of his open eyes were widely dilated.

Gates, not entirely unmoved, watched the struggling subside into a deathlike stillness, and the rigid jaw relax. With a growing fear that he had used too many of the deadly nightshade berries, he bent anxiously over the prostrate figure. But the heart under the gray flannel shirt was beating strongly, and after taking away the arsenal of weapons which bulged from every pocket he prepared to make their quarters more comfortable.

Before unconsciousness had changed to delirium the tent had been set up, and Mosby had been dragged under its protecting cover.

And then Gates sat down to wait and watch. He had no medicines, except what virtue lay in plenty of cold water. For twenty-four hours Mosby raged in delirium, tearing at the ropes that tied him, singing snatches of ribald songs interspersed with oaths. Then the fever abated, and left him, weak, sullen, and entirely conscious. He followed Gates with vindictive eyes as he moved about the camp, but he made no effort to escape.

The third day saw a great improvement in his condition. Gates prepared to break camp and start back over the trail again, Mosby watching his preparations with evident anxiety.

"Loose these ropes, can't you?" he growled surlily. "I'm tied that tight I can't even take a drink without you feedin' it to me like a baby."

Gates smiled a little and shook his head. But he brought a tin of fresh water from the spring and held it to the other man's lips. Mosby drank, his mocking eyes fixed on Gates, then with a quick jerk of his head he pushed the cup aside and spit the water full in the younger man's face. Gates wiped it off coolly.

"I guess you're well enough to travel," he said. "I'd better get you off my hands soon, or I may forget and kill you."

"You white-livered specimen hunter—you're afraid to shoot," taunted Mosby.

But Gates still controlled himself.

The camp kit having been packed, they took up their homeward march. Mosby was leading, with his arms tied behind him. That night Mosby slept, while Gates watched him unremittingly.

The following day they reached the spot where below in the valley lay the extemporized camp. But much to Mosby's surprise his captor seemed as anxious as he himself to avoid discovery. They passed unseen, however, and plunged into the secure depths of the forest behind. For a time they traveled in silence. Then Mosby halted and turned. "What's your game?" he said roughly. "Why didn't you sing out back there?"

"Well," said Gates, with a half smile, "it's precisely my game to see that those fellows don't get you. I'm the sheriff."

The Death Trap

PAUL GALLICO

I went back today and looked at a diary I wrote thirty years ago and put away in the bottom of an old theatrical trunk. It was the account of the end of the Great Armando. And I got out something else, too, and looked at it again for the first time since it had come into my hands so long ago. It was a canvas straitjacket with leather straps, the metal buckles rusted from contact with the waters of the Detroit River.

Still sewed into the sleeves was the gimmick, that simple and devilish device of a mean and murderous man which, I wrote in my diary back in 1925, destroyed the Great Armando as surely as a bullet in the brain or a knife stuck in his heart. Only we never found his body afterward.

The Great Armando was a farm boy from Perrysville, Ohio, whose real name was Joe Ferris. I was his partner for five years and loved him like a brother. He was a queer, brave, moody fellow whose father was American and his mother Polish. He was the strongest man I ever knew, particularly in his fingers, hands, and wrists.

He wasn't even a big guy, being no more than five foot ten and stocky, with shoulders and chest like a barrel. And I guess the most important thing in the world to him was the legend we'd built up about his escapes. He boasted that there wasn't a prison cell, manacle, lock, or restraint that could hold him.

And it was true, in a way. He was the greatest showman I ever knew, with piercing black eyes and a big shock of black hair. When in public, he talked with some kind of accent he'd picked up from a Mexican knife thrower during his carny days. But in private with me, he was as American as chewing gum, Cornflakes, and batting averages.

When he was a kid, a carnival came through Perrysville and he ran away with it from his old man's farm. He picked up everything good and bad a kid can learn around a carnival, but when he met an Australian who taught him to escape from rope ties, he found his life's work. Thereafter, he concentrated on escapes and worked up a fair living with an act devoted to getting out of rope ties, straitjackets, handcuffs, and so on.

But he didn't become the Great Armando and hit the big money until I joined up with him in 1920, after the war. If that's blowing my own horn, Joe Ferris would have been the first to acknowledge it. It just happened I had what he needed to take him out of the class of the mediocre performers barnstorming the country with cheap carnivals and put him in the ranks of the world's great illusionists whose names will never be forgotten, like Robert Houdin, Herrmann the Great, Thurston, Harry Kellar, and Harry Houdini.

My name is Carl Hegemeyer, master mechanic and locksmith. My father came over from Germany in 1888. He taught me the accumulated knowledge of eight generations of locksmiths, which could also be summed up in the sentence: anything that can be locked can likewise be opened, provided you have the right key or instrument.

But I had another accomplishment that made me indispensable to the myth of the Great Armando. I could look at a key and several hours later duplicate it from memory. When we traveled around, I had the finest little portable, power-driven metal lathe and key cutter with me. I could plug it into any hotel-room outlet or in emergencies run it off the battery in our car.

An hour or so after a preliminary conference on any escape challenge at which I saw the key used to lock the device, Armando would have a duplicate. Concealing it was no problem for a man with his training in sleight of hand.

There's no such thing as magic. You know that. You've seen a lot of magic shows from out front where the magician performs the apparently impossible. Well, it not only seems impossible—it is. There's a gaff to everything.

Gaff is the carnival word for the gimmick, the trick, the concealed device, the common-sense explanation of how it is done. Usually the gaff is something so simple you don't

want to believe it. You'd see the Great Armando buried
handcuffed in a stone sarcophagus, and three minutes later
he'd be out of it, taking his bow. Common sense would tell
you he couldn't do it unless he had superhuman powers
or assistance. But the kind of showmanship he'd give you
would make you want to believe in the superhuman powers.
That's what you paid your money for.

Yet, in nine cases out of ten, he had assistance. I provided
it. With my help, he escaped from a sealed subway caisson,
a time vault in the National Bank, a 4000-year-old Greek stone
coffin, the punishment cell at Alcatraz, and countless types of
manacles and restraining jackets.

But don't forget, he had moxie along with it. Even if you
know the gimmicks, it takes guts to let them lace you into a
straitjacket, stuff you into a Government mailbag and padlock it, nail you into a packing case bound with rope, and
drop you into an icy river in midwinter.

The only one to come near the Great Armando was
Houdini, and everything Houdini did, Armando did better.
Houdini did the river-escape trick, only he used handcuffs
that he could get out of in ten seconds. Nobody but Armando
dared to do it wearing the straitjacket and letting an expert
truss him up.

Yet, as I wrote in my diary, the straitjacket finished him,
leastways, the gimmick in it. And a woman put it there,
the only woman he ever loved.

He was a queer duck, was Joe Ferris. Nobody ever knew
him or got close to him, not even I, and I was his trusted
partner. I suppose that was the Polish in him. Often he was
moody and suspicious. He kept his money stashed away in
cash in safe-deposit boxes under different names that I never

even knew. He thought only of his reputation and the myth of the Great Armando. He said to me, "Remember this. Whatever happens, the Great Armando never fails."

Yet he was no fool either and knew the risks he was running. "The first time I get a real bad scare," he once told me, "I'll quit and nobody'll ever hear of the Great Armando again. But up to now, I haven't seen anything we can't beat."

But that was before we met up with Sheriff Jules Massin, of Ossowo County, in the tough River Rouge section of Detroit, where we were doing the water escape as preliminary publicity to Armando's being booked into the Michigan Palace Theater in Detroit. The sheriff had taken up our challenge to lace Armando into a straitjacket from which he could not escape.

On the face of it, it was routine. There was no straitjacket made that Armando couldn't get out of in less than a minute. But we never took chances. Armando would not guarantee to get out of any restraining device unless he could inspect it first. The padlock on the mail sack had to be closed and opened in our presence. This gave me the necessary gander at the key. And the packing case had to go on exhibition in the lobby of the theater before and after the stunt. That's when we gaffed it. We thought we had every angle covered. Only we never figured to come up against a man with murder in his heart.

There was a crowd in the sheriff's office the day we went there to inspect the restraints and set up the stunt—deputies, detectives, police, reporters, and photographers. The sheriff's wife was there too. His office was on the ground floor of his home. At first I didn't notice her. She had a scarf bound around her head, European style. She had pale cheeks and prominent eyes that seemed absolutely devoid of expression.

They did not even flicker when the sheriff, noticing her in the forefront of those crowding around his desk, snarled, "What are you doin' here, Tina? Can't you see I'm busy?"

She was submissive to his abuse. Every line of her body proclaimed her to be cowed and hopeless. Yet she did not go, and soon other matters claimed the sheriff's attention.

The sheriff was a mean man. Mean, dirty, and dangerous. He wasn't a copper for nothing. He liked it. We meet all kinds in our racket, from plain smart alecks who think it is fun to make a monkey out of a performer, to cops and jailers who don't like to see you make a monkey out of them. But we'd never run up against a guy nursing murder in his heart because it was for free. Armando always signed a release.

That was the sheriff. I knew him for a killer—a killer inside the law—from the moment I walked into his office. He was over six feet tall, fat, burly, and dirty. His clothes were dirty, his skin, his fingernails, and his teeth. His breath was bad. He wore a fancy gun in a belt holster. You could see he loved the power it gave him.

Massin threw a straitjacket onto his desk and sneered, "Anything wrong with that?"

It was an ordinary violence-restraint jacket with straps and buckles, the easiest type for Armando, for the canvas was not unusually thick. No matter how strong the manipulator, Armando, by swelling his muscles, could always reserve enough slack to get his arms over his head. Then he opened the buckles through the canvas. I told you he had the most powerful fingers in the world. In that department he was superhuman. That's why he was called great.

I picked up the jacket to show Armando. But he wasn't looking. Something strange had happened. He was staring instead at Tina Massin, and on his face was an expression such as I had never seen there before.

I had to catch my breath. Her headcloth had fallen back upon her neck, revealing her blond hair and the perfect oval of her face. She looked like the pale, imprisoned princess in the book of Grimm's fairy tales I had when I was a kid. The impression she made upon me at that moment was one I could never forget.

Have you ever known it to happen that you see someone for the first time and in that moment you know that person's life story almost as though you had read it in a book? She was of foreign extraction, maybe Polish or Finnish. I guessed she had been taken from an institution or orphanage into the sheriff's establishment as household drudge. She had no doubt been first abused and later married because it was more convenient to own a wife than a servant. There are some women who become the hopeless, submissive captives of the most appalling men. Such a one was Tina Massin.

They were caught up in each other's eyes, these two utterly different and contrasting strangers, the showman with the long black hair and piercing glance, the pale girl with the thick silken hair, and eyes that were for the first time alive and filled with a kind of pleading. Any moment it would become obvious that two people had found each other, had fallen in love, and were attempting to communicate.

I created a diversion by tossing the jacket back onto the desk. "That's O.K.," I said.

The sheriff sniggered unpleasantly. "It's the way I strap

'em into it," he said. I was satisfied to let Armando deal with
that. The post-office inspector produced the mailbag. I bent
over to examine the thickness, fittings, and padlock. I had a
dozen keys that would open it. Armando would have two of
them concealed on his person, attached to a fine wire. Once
out of the straitjacket—a matter of sixty seconds—he would
push out the key and manipulate it, again through the
material of the sack.

It was O.K. Nevertheless, I made them open and shut the
lock several times to make sure it hadn't been gaffed with shot
or sand. Mrs. Massin dropped her handkerchief. Armando
stooped to pick it up, as did she. Their fingers touched for
an instant. I was still bent over, examining the mailbag.

I heard her whisper to him, "For heaven's sake, don't do
it."

The time set was ten the next morning at the Western and
Lakes Railroad pier, where there was a big traveling crane.
The document releasing the sheriff's office and Detroit police
from all responsibility was produced and the photographers
jostled for position. Somebody handed Armando a pen. Mrs.
Massin made a slight gesture with her hand. Their eyes met
once more. She licked dry lips and, almost imperceptibly,
shook her head. The sheriff missed the byplay, but sniggered
again.

"Going to welsh?" he asked. Then, addressing everyone in
general, he said, "I say all greasers are yellow."

Joe Ferris flourished the pen dramatically. "Armando he
nevaire welsh," he said, and signed.

Tina Massin's eyes were extinguished. All the life went
from her. She was hopeless, despairing, submissive. She
turned and went out of the room.

I went to see Harry Hopp, an old-time reporter friend on the *Free Press*. I told you we never left anything to chance. I didn't like the setup for two cents.

I asked, "What's the background on your fragrant sheriff of Ossowo County?"

Hopp said, "Can't tell you anything good about him. And as long as you're asking, he hates carnivals and the carny crowd. They can't get the time of day in his county. You better watch out for that baby."

"Yeah," I said. "I got that. But why?"

"Shakedown," he replied. "There was a carnival through here five years ago really loaded with grift. They shelled out plenty to the sheriff to operate, but when he came back again for a second handout, they beat him up and threw him out. Maybe your boy friend even was with that carny and saw it happen. Massin's death on anything connected with traveling shows or midways."

That night I said to Armando, "Listen, Joe. Were you ever with a grift show that beat up a sheriff around here before you started in with me?"

He reflected, and then said slowly, "So that's where I know him from. When he tried to shake me down, I poked him, and that started it."

I said, "I don't like it. He's got it in for you. Let's call it off. We can do it in Cleveland next week."

He looked at me as if I were out of my mind, and asked, "Have we got all the angles covered?"

I went back over things in my mind. There was nothing that could happen that we hadn't thought of. "Yes," I said.

"O.K.," he said, "we go. We can't afford to back out."

But I was wrong. There was something I hadn't thought of,

something so simple and elementary as a means of destroying Armando that it never dawned on me until it was too late.

The day of the test was damp, cold, and sunless. There were chunks of ice floating in the river. In spite of the raw, blustery weather, the pier and several adjoining piers were black with people. We'd had a big press in advance of the attempt.

The stunt was routine, and we'd done it a dozen times before. The gaff was this: as soon as they started to nail the cover onto the box, Armando would begin working his way out of the straitjacket and the mailbag, while I'd stall, suggesting putting in more nails or tying the rope tighter, until I got a signal from Armando that he was free of the restraints. The crate had been gimmicked by us the night before with a concealed sliding panel in one side. Fifteen seconds after the box disappeared beneath the surface, he'd be out of it.

It was that simple, like all stage or escape illusions, except it was the way Armando did it that made it look so good. It is a part of the showmanship in that kind of act that when you really think a guy is in danger he's as safe as he'd be at home in bed. The real deadly stuff doesn't show. Like staying under, holding your breath for more than three minutes in freezing water, and then coming up amidst ice floes or risking being carried away under the ice by the current. He had a right to call himself the Great Armando and to be proud of his rep.

When Armando and I arrived, there was a big bunch of reporters, including Harry Hopp and several sob sisters, and a horde of photographers and newsreel men. Captain Harry Stevens, of the river police, was giving directions to a police launch that was to pick Armando up if and when he appeared. He was not too pleased at being used for a publicity stunt and greeted us sourly.

He said, "O.K., O.K. Let's get going and get out of here. You fellows signed a release, didn't you?"

Sheriff Massin, wearing a big sheepskin-lined coat, said, "Yup. Got it right here."

Armando slipped out of his cloak. Underneath, he was wearing trousers and sweat shirt of light, warm wool and sneakers. The sheriff stepped over with the straitjacket, a nasty, self-satisfied smile on his face. Tina Massin was there in the front row. She wasn't pretty anymore. Her face was tearstained and filled with fear. Her eyes were fixed upon the jacket.

I spotted something about the sleeves that had not been there the day before. My stomach started to sink. I said, "Here, wait a minute. Let me see that jacket. It's been gimmicked."

The sheriff said, "They're stalling," but handed it over.

I turned out the sleeves. Inside, to the canvas lining, had been sewed ten finger grips of plaited strips of colored straw. You've seen them in any magic or trick store or child's magic set. Once they are slipped over a finger, the harder you pull the more tightly they grip. The device also is used commercially for hoisting, and there is no possible way of tearing loose from it. The secret of escape is to push against the grips. The plaits then contract and enlarge so that the finger can be removed. But fastened inside the long narrow sleeve of the jacket, there was no leverage to push. And deprived of the use of his fingers, the Great Armando was as good as dead.

I saw Armando's eyes narrow when he saw the fatal trap, and the sweat beads form on his upper lip and under his eyes. It was the first time I ever saw Joe Ferris afraid.

I said, "What's this? Those things weren't in there yesterday when we inspected the jacket."

Massin said, "Well, they're in there now."

Tina Massin seemed about to faint. I had a picture of her sitting up all night, with the sheriff standing over her, sewing in those terrible devices designed to kill a man for free.

Captain Stevens came over, took the straitjacket, and looked at it and the innocent-looking toy finger grips plaited in reds, yellows, greens, and purples. "What's the idea, sheriff?" he asked.

Massin bustled truculently and replied loudly, so that all the press could hear. "This greaser says he can get out of anything, don't he? I had a feller once I hadda take to the loony house. Killed three guys. He got out of the jacket. He had hands like a gorilla. I fixed him up like this. He didn't get out. O.K., so let this greaseball put up or shut up. They seen them kind of grips a dozen times before in their racket."

Captain Stevens looked doubtful, but I could sense that he was secretly pleased, in a way, that a performer who had put them to a lot of needless trouble was going to be shown up. He said to us, "What about it, boys? You don't have to go through with it if you don't want to, but make up your minds and let's get out of here."

Harry Hopp, the *Free Press* reporter, said, "Don't let him do it, Carl. It's sheer murder. I'll see that he doesn't get the worst of it in the papers."

Massin laughed his loud, dirty laugh. "I knew the four-flusher would welsh."

"Welsh nothing!" I shouted. "Our contract clearly stated. . . ."

"Quiet, everyone!" It was Armando. And even in that crisis he didn't forget the phony Mexican accent. "Shut up, Carl."

But he wasn't looking at me. He was looking straight at Tina Massin and she at him. There was no mistake. They were in love all right. They had found and lost each other in the same moment. They were saying good-by, for there was no hope for them. She was the wife of a brute who would never let her go. And he was faced with an insoluble dilemma. Because if he went through with the stunt he was a dead man. And if he backed out he might as well be dead, because he would never again be the Great Armando.

He said, "All right, sheriff, I am ready."

The sheriff stepped forward, laughing. "So long, sucker. You asked for it." Things moved fast then as he went about his for-free murder, forcing each finger of Armando's hands deep into the plaits of the straw finger grips, then pushing his knee into Armando's back in order to haul the straps tighter.

And all the time Joe Ferris continued to look only on the white face of this girl he had come to love in such a strange manner, and who had been forced to become his executioner. Her eyes were lost in his. Her lips moved, though no sound came, but I would have sworn they were communicating for the last time.

When four men lifted the mail sack, with Armando inside it, into the packing case and the electric crane traveled over and lowered the lid onto the top, Tina Massin gave a soft cry and crumpled to the pier in a dead faint.

The sheriff laughed, saying, "Now what's the matter with her?"

A newsreel cameraman shouted, "Hey, sheriff, will ya look out? You're in the way of the shot!" I felt as if it were I who was going to die.

I jumped up onto the box to stall as long at I could and give him a chance, even though I knew it was hopeless. There was no signal from him as usual, to let me know he was out of the jacket and sack, waiting for the plunge with his finger on the gaffed panel that would slide open and free him as soon as he sank beneath the surface.

Then he hadn't got out. The child's toy had defeated him. The legend of the Great Armando was a thing of the past. But I was determined to save the life of Joe Ferris.

The sheriff cried, "Lower away!" and there was a cheer from the crowd as the steel cable payed out. The weighted crate went in with a splash and began to settle as the water poured in through the interstices.

I had a sickening vision of Armando trussed up like a mummy in the horrid canvas jacket, his fingers helplessly trapped in the straw grips, the icy water pouring into the case, the mail sack filling up, his last gasp for oxygen. Then the hopeless last-minute struggle, tugging against the inexorable grips, and the final bubble bursting from the tortured lungs. After that, silence.

Air was rushing up in a dirty surface swirl as the case sank with its burden. When my stopwatch showed two minutes and there was no sign of an arm or dark head breaking the gray river surface, I bawled in panic. "Haul away! Get him up out of there! Something's gone wrong! Get him up, do you hear!"

There was some confused shouting, and I could see the

police captain bawling futilely at the man in the operator's hanging booth of the crane. But there was no rattle of machinery or running of steel cable over the wheel. Something had happened to the crane or the power, for I could see the operator wrestling with his levers.

I went over the side of the pier into the water. Men and women were screaming. I had a crazy idea I could swim down, work the panel, and get him out of there, sack and all, and up to the surface. I fought the cable and my bursting lungs. Then the police launch came and fished me out. After ten minutes, the power came on again and the crate was raised. But there was not a chance in the world that the Great Armando was still alive. The sheriff had won.

Workmen attacked the case with axes and crowbars. Interns from an ambulance, their white trousers showing beneath their dark overcoats, stood by with their equipment. With a splintering and wrenching, the side of the case broke away, revealing the locked mail sack.

And I was the first one to see that it wasn't full enough! With a yell, I broke away from Harry Hopp, seized the key from the postal inspector, and opened the padlock.

It was empty! No, not quite empty. Inside, buckled as though it had never been unfastened, the terrible finger grips still in place, was the straitjacket neatly folded. But of the Great Armando there was no sign. He had accomplished his greatest escape!

It was his last, too, for he was never seen again. The police dredged, grappled, and dived for three days, but his body was never recovered. He had defeated the vicious finger grips, the jacket, the mail sack, and the case, and got out, and then, perhaps at the last moment, exhausted from the struggle, his strength gone, he had drowned and been swept downriver or under a pier.

I went to a hospital myself with pneumonia. They said in my delirium I swore I'd kill Sheriff Massin for murdering my friend and partner. It turned out that it wasn't necessary. Six months after the disappearance of the Great Armando I read in a newspaper that Jules Massin was shot to death in a saloon by the saloonkeeper he had attempted to shake down. I never heard what became of Mrs. Massin after that.

A couple of months after I got out of the hospital, Captain Stevens, of the river police, sent me the straitjacket, complete with the sheriff's deadly gaff, as a souvenir. I couldn't bear to look at it and put it away, with my diary of how it all happened, in the bottom of my trunk. Then I went back into the locksmith business.

All that was thirty years ago. Now I am holding the jacket in my fingers again. For two days ago I saw Joe Ferris, the Great Armando! And with him was Tina Massin! I'll swear it! I couldn't have been mistaken even though his hair was white and his features changed. She looked almost the same, except happy. It happened when I was coming out of a movie house in Athens, Georgia.

I said, "Joe! Joe Ferris! And Tina Massin!"

They denied it. They stopped politely, but their expressions remained blank.

The man said, "You must be mistaking us for someone else. My name is Vernon Howard, and this is Mrs. Howard here. I'm in the grain-and-feed business. Anyone in Athens knows me. And now, if you'll excuse Mrs. Howard and me. . . ."

Vernon Howard's Grain and Feed Store was at the corner of the Boulevard and Pecan Street. When I instituted inquiries as to how long it had been there, the invariable answer was, "Oh, 'bout as long as I kin remember." But when I got down to cases, no one seemed to remember them back for thirty years or longer.

When I returned to New York, I dug out the straitjacket of Sheriff Massin. I hadn't touched it since the day I thought it had killed the Great Armando. The color on the finger grips of plaited straw had run, but otherwise they were exactly as they had been on that fatal day. I examined them. Then I took a magnifying glass. I tried them out by putting my fingers in and yanking. They pulled loose. And after that I knew the secret of how the Great Armando had escaped from the inescapable trap laid for him by vindictive Sheriff Massin. The finger stalls had been subtly and efficiently gaffed by his wife. The straw plaits had been cut with scissors in such a way as to defy casual inspection, but in every case destroying the tension of the plaits, so that they no longer pulled against one another.

I remembered the look between them, the money he had stashed away in safe-deposit boxes, and his remark, "If I ever get a real scare, I'll quit and nobody'll ever hear of the Great Armando again." And how easily he could have swum ashore under cover of the excitement and vanished, to return when he read Sheriff Massin was dead.

Yeah, we'd thought of everything, except one thing. And in the end it was Joe Ferris, the Great Armando, who had the guts to put his faith in love as a gimmick.

The Letter of the Law

DON KNOWLTON

The facts, as reported in the Hartville *Clarion*, were as follows.

John Skoda, twenty-three, his wife Mary, twenty-one, and their infant daughter Anna, lived in a small rented house at 371 Ash Street. Rooming next door was Joe Kryslak, thirty-three, unmarried, and, for the most part, unemployed.

Kryslak had been forcing his attentions on Skoda's wife, and Skoda had been heard to say to Kryslak, "I'll kill you if I ever find you in my house again."

On July 17, when Skoda came home from the garage where

he worked (carrying a big wrench in his pocket), a neighbor woman called out to him, "Kryslak's inside your house, and he's drunk."

Skoda ran into his house to find furniture overturned, the baby on the floor, and his wife trying to push off Kryslak. Skoda jerked the wrench from his pocket, swung it hard, hit Kryslak on the back of the head, and killed him. The neighbor woman, standing in the door, saw it.

Skoda then ran to his car and headed out of town. He was picked up for speeding before it was even known that he was wanted for murder. . . .

The case had come up before Judge Harrison Bentley, of the Court of Common Pleas. The judge was, in a way, the leading citizen of Hartville. There were men in the town with more money; there were men who were more brilliant; but for correctness in all respects and for utter integrity, there was no one in Hartville who approached the judge.

On the bench he was an imposing figure. He was not a large man, but his chiseled features, set off by coal-black hair, gave an impression almost of majesty. The very way in which he wore his horn-rimmed glasses seemed indicative of deep learning. Here, one felt, was the Law—fair, impartial, omnipotent, inexorable.

All his life the judge had done the right things. He was graduated at the top of his class. He had married a girl of excellent social position and considerable property. In building up a law practice he had scrupulously refrained from the defense of unsavory characters. He had no children, but was active in school matters. At social events he would take a cocktail, but only one. He gave to charity, generously but not ostentatiously.

His philosophy as to the law was simple. Principles that evolved over the years, with the aid of many generations of legal brains, became crystallized into statutes that were to be accepted and obeyed. A law was definitive. It did not say "perhaps," or "probably," or "in most cases." The penalties for infringement of the law were likewise defined. Therefore, all a judge had to do, to be right, was to know the law and stick with it, and to it.

By the close of the afternoon of Friday, October 19, all the evidence in the Skoda case was in. The prosecution and the defense had rested. On Saturday the judge played golf with Oscar Begg, President of the First National Bank. The judge's game was not very good. Of course, Begg kept talking about the proposed municipal bond issue, but that was not what made it difficult for the judge to keep his eye on the ball. On Monday he would have to summarize, and charge the jury, in the Skoda murder trial. His brain was turning round and round, seeking to formulate the exact wording he should use.

Of course the man was guilty. The only question was whether the verdict would be murder or manslaughter.

The prosecution had claimed that Skoda had brought home that heavy wrench with the premeditated intent of killing Kryslak with it, if he found him in his home, as Skoda had actually threatened to do.

The defense had claimed that Skoda had brought the wrench home to repair the plumbing in his kitchen, and that hitting Kryslak with it had been an unpremeditated act, committed instinctively, without intent to kill, and under circumstances so compelling that any husband would under-stand.

But Skoda had fled. He had run away. This, the prosecu-tion maintained, presumed consciousness of guilt.

Judge Bentley sliced another drive and sent it far into the rough. Oh, well, he thought, as he struggled through nettles and wild sunflowers to a thorn-apple thicket, it is up to the jury to decide. All I have to do is to give them clear in-structions as to the distinction between murder and man-slaughter, and define the sentences, mandatory or permissive, as set forth in the statutes.

But he was not in a good frame of mind. There kept rising before him the picture of Mary Skoda, as she sat in the court-room, with her baby daughter on her lap.

"Confound these nettles," he said, flailing about with his mashie, hunting for the ball. Oscar Begg came over to help.

They stood under a black-walnut tree. The leaves were off, but the big green spheres of the nuts, in their shucks, still clung in clusters on the branches.

"Ever gather them, when you were a boy?" asked Oscar.

Forty years fell off Judge Bentley's shoulders. He sat down on a log, and instantly he was back on his grandfather's farm, on the big slope northwest of the barn. There were other boys there too, boys whose names he had long since for-gotten. One of them shook the nuts from the tree. The rest gathered them in piles, and then knocked off the outer shucks with wooden clubs and put the nuts in a basket. Fingers were stained a rich, deep brown. And the smell— that pungent fragrance of October.

Judge Bentley picked up a fallen walnut in its shuck and sniffed deeply. Oscar Begg sat down too.

"Like black walnuts?" the banker asked.

The judge was too full of recollections—and something else he could not quite understand—to speak. He merely nodded.

"I've got a big black-walnut tree in the back of my yard that is loaded," Oscar went on. "Never saw such a crop. We won't want them. My wife and I are leaving town tonight and will be gone for two weeks. Come over and get them if you want to."

The judge did not find his ball. He put down another, and on the third swing he got back on the fairway. But he was still back on his grandfather's farm.

The next morning the illusion still persisted. He could almost hear his grandfather calling the cows, and he could almost smell the salt pork sizzling on the stove.

The judge lived not far from the courthouse, on an old but most desirable street, shaded by spreading elms. The yard backed up to a creek that ran parallel with the street. The little stream was clear and unpolluted. The brush and the trees on its banks had been allowed to grow.

On Sunday morning the judge and his wife sat opposite each other in the half-breakfast room, half-greenhouse that looked out over the backyard and the creek. They were lingering over eggs and coffee.

"We'd better get started," his wife said. "If we're going to get to the Richards by one."

"I don't think I care to go," said the judge, unexpectedly.

"Now, Harrison, the Stapletons will be there and the Hardings. . . ."

"I'm sorry," said her husband flatly, "but I'm not going. I'm just not in the mood."

But he persuaded his wife to go, and she took the car and headed north, to the Richards' house party. At the last minute she decided to make a trip of it and go on to visit other friends the next day. The judge—it being Sunday, with no day help around the house—was left alone. Alone, with an inexplicable unrest in his system, and a nostalgic yearning to recapture a day, even an hour, of forty years ago.

He stepped to the edge of the creek behind the house and looked down. The sunshine filtering through the haze highlighted the autumn browns of the beeches and the reds of the maples. There were dancing colors in the weeds and in the grass. The milkweed pods had exploded into fluffs of white. Every branch, every stalk, seemed endowed with a magic of its own. And Judge Bentley could have sworn that he smelled black walnuts, as plain as plain could be.

"Well, why not?" he asked suddenly, aloud. Oscar Begg's house also backed up to the creek, a short distance downstream from the Bentley house. To reach Begg's backyard the judge had only to follow the footpath through the brush alongside the creek.

A basket? No, a bag would be better. In his basement he found an old burlap sack.

But what should he wear? The trouble was that he literally did not have any old clothes; his wife always got rid of them. Then he remembered. Hanging in the garage was a torn pair of pants left by the gardener, and a ragged coat. In the attic he found a pair of old camping shoes. Further digging uncovered a moth-eaten felt hat. Arrayed in these, the judge looked at himself in the glass.

Gone was the judge, the dignified, majestic figure of the Law. There stood before him, in the mirror, a most disreputable-looking character. Suddenly he felt like a boy let out of school. Then it came to him. Should he go all the way? Why not? Nobody would see him, walking down the footpath, screened by the brush. Nobody would notice him in Oscar Begg's backyard. The Beggs were away from home.

The judge took off his horn-rimmed glasses. Except for fine print, he could see quite well without them. He took out his false teeth—they always did annoy him. Then he removed his toupee. There was not a soul in Hartville, except the judge's wife, who knew that he was as bald as a baby. He had guarded the secret well.

With the moth-eaten hat jammed down on his head and the burlap bag over his shoulder, the judge started down the path that followed the stream.

In a few moments he came on a patch of fall asters, frost flowers, his grandmother used to call them. The pattern of purple starlets against the brown background of fallen leaves held him silent and wondering. There had been such a clump of asters behind the icehouse at the old farm. The plank walk, the pear tree, the grindstone, every detail flashed clear in his memory. Purple and brown, asters and leaves— why should he think at that moment of Mary Skoda and her baby? Judge Bentley sighed and went on down the path.

Oscar Begg's black-walnut tree was indeed loaded. The ground was covered with nuts, but there were also plenty still on the tree. It had not occurred to the judge that he might climb the tree. But that was the proper procedure. Any boy knew that. The tree branched low. Going up would be as simple as mounting a ladder.

Up went the judge. For a few precious, fleeting moments he was just ten years old. He stomped on one branch after another and reveled in the music of the nuts falling to the ground below. He was just about to step to an even higher perch when a yell came from beneath the tree.

The judge looked down. Looking up into the tree was a policeman. "What do you think you're doing?"

"Getting walnuts," replied the judge, feeling silly. As he climbed down out of the tree a woman came running from the adjoining yard.

"That's him!" she said to the officer. "It's him all right. I can tell by his clothes, but I'd know him anyway."

The judge reached the ground and said to the officer, "Now what is this all about?"

"You're asking *me*?" said the policeman. "I'm asking *you*."

"I told you. I'm gathering walnuts."

"What you're doing," said the officer, "is trespassing and stealing property."

"But you don't understand," said the judge. "Mr. Begg told me I could come and take these nuts."

"Baloney," interrupted the officer. "Are you sure, Mrs. Kilroy?"

"Of course, I'm sure," she said. "He's the man who was trying to break into my house yesterday. That's when I called you, so when I saw him again today I phoned."

"Wait a minute!" broke in the judge. "Madam, with all due respect to your sincerity, you are completely mistaken. I realize, officer, that you deserve an explanation. I'm a neighbor and a friend of Mr. Begg's. I live just up the street. Mr. Begg and his wife have gone out of town, and he suggested to me that I might like to have some of these walnuts. That's all there is to it."

The policeman gave him a withering glance. "Oh, so you live just up the street, eh?" he said mockingly.

"Yes! Why, you know me. I'm Judge Bentley, of the Common Pleas Court."

The policeman wagged his head sadly from side to side. "Well, if that doesn't beat everything!" he said. "A bald-headed old tramp like you trying to pass himself off as Judge Bentley!"

In a panic the judge reached for his hat. It wasn't there! It had fallen off while he was in the tree.

The judge said not another word. Oh, he could protest to high heaven. He could demand that the officer summon the clerk of the court, or the bailiff, or other people who could confirm his identity. But that was unthinkable. For in that case he would stand revealed without his teeth and his toupee! The only possible safety—for the moment, at least —lay in the officer continuing to assume that he was not, could not *possibly* be, Judge Bentley.

"Mrs. Kilroy," said the officer, "while I hold him here, would you mind calling the station and telling them to send out the wagon?"

Swiftly the officer stepped forward and frisked the judge's pockets. They were empty.

When the police car came, they rode in silence to the station. There the man at the desk looked up in inquiry.

"Prowler," explained the officer who had made the arrest. "Vagrant, probably. No identification on him. Caught stealing nuts. Suspected of housebreaking. Better put him away until tomorrow morning."

The judge stiffened. At 9 a.m. the next morning he was

supposed to be on the bench, charging the jury in the Skoda case.

"What shall we book him on?" asked the man at the desk.

"Darned if I know," answered the officer. "Suspicious character, I guess. I think he's loony. He says he's Judge Bentley."

"What!" The man at the desk laughed loudly.

"Come to think of it," he said finally, "he does look a bit like the judge. It's a scream."

They took him to the jail. It was, ironically enough, in the basement of the courthouse.

The cell in which they put him already had an occupant, a man with enormous shoulders, clad in a ragged red sweater and faded corduroy pants.

"Welcome to the abode of the transgressors," said the big man. "What are you in for, Mac?"

The judge made no answer. He had some hard thinking to do. The situation was impossible!

Judge Bentley, *in jail,* in tramp's clothes, minus hair and teeth, charged with nut stealing and housebreaking. What a story for the newspapers! How the town would laugh! Toupee—ha, ha, ha! Oh, that would be the end, the very end. He would never be able to hold up his head again.

But unless he had them phone someone to come and identify him, how could he get out of jail and appear in court next morning? What if he didn't appear? The jury would take their seats. The bailiff would prepare to open court, and lo, no judge!

They would phone his home—no answer, his wife was not due back until Wednesday. They would go to his house and find that his bed had not been slept in. Judge Bentley missing! The news would go out over the air. It would make headlines. And then?

Round and round on the treadmill, and the judge could find no satisfactory answer, no answer that would save him from public humiliation.

Hours later there was a sudden rattle at the door. A little man pushed two supper trays into the cell and departed.

"Well, Mac," said the big man in the red sweater, "if you won't talk maybe you'll eat."

Absently the judge looked at his tray.

"Beans again," observed the big man.

Mechanically the judge, toothless, went through the motions of eating.

"Look," said the judge's cell mate. "I've been cooped up here for three days with nobody to talk to. It was all right for Byron to say 'there is society where none intrudes,' but that was on the seashore, not in jail. It gets tough in here, all by yourself."

The judge looked up in surprise.

"Man is a gregarious animal," the man went on. "It isn't human for you to just sit there, hour after hour, like Rodin's 'Thinker.' Let us talk! You be Johnson and I'll be Boswell, or vice versa, if you prefer. I care not what paltry offense you have committed against society. From the looks of you, I'd guess you were merely trying, in your small way, to bring about a more equitable distribution of wealth. Am I right?"

"I was just trying to get something to eat," said the judge.

"Then they may not make it too tough for you. But I don't know. The judge in this town is a holy terror."

"Is that so?" asked the judge.

"He knows not the quality of mercy. He cares only for facts and figures. In his scheme of things there is no place for human frailty. It ought not to exist. The word *sympathy* is not in his vocabulary."

"How do you know so much about him?" asked the judge. "Did you ever see him in court?"

"No, I've never seen Bloodless Bentley, as they call him, but I know a lot about him. You see, I am—or rather, I was —a linotype operator on the Kane City *Blade*. You know Kane City? It's only ten miles from here. Well, I typeset all the *Blade*'s stories about the trials here. And unlike most typographers I read what I set. In fact, I read everything I can lay my hands on—and I drink. That's my trouble, reading and drinking."

The big man sighed. "Old Bentley may let *you* off with ten days," he went on, "but *me*—I'll get the book. Driving while intoxicated. Not just drunk—pie-eyed, plastered, absolutely pifflicated. What that old Puritan will do to me. . . ."

He drew his finger across his throat. "I would have been up before him by now, but he's been on a murder case. Oh, well! 'This, too, will pass.' "

The big man smiled unexpectedly. It lit up a peculiarly ugly face. "Cheer up, Mac," he said, "suppose we *had* been righteous, rich, and famous? 'The paths of glory lead but to the grave.' But I *am* darned tired of waiting in this cell."

He began pacing up and down. "Oh," he mused, "I suppose we have to have laws and judges and all that sort of thing, but I have often reflected upon the tyranny of justice."

In spite of his predicament the judge's mounting curiosity got the better of him. "What do you mean by that, the tyranny of justice?" he asked.

"The law," said the big man, "of necessity groups offenses in categories and provides specific penalties. This is all right in theory, but the whole system is based on averages and may not properly apply to any individual case. There are moral principles that at times should take precedence over the letter of the law, and for this the law makes no allowances. The law says this, the law says that. We are caught in the strait-jacket of the law."

"But don't you see—"

"Here's what I mean. Under the law a man who robs a store to get money so that his sick child can have the doctor is just as guilty, and deserves exactly the same penalty, as a man who robs a bank to get money to buy a chorus girl champagne."

"But—"

"I say," the big man kept on, "that justice should give due consideration to circumstances. Now take my case, for instance."

The judge had almost revealed himself as not being what he appeared to be. Just in time he settled back to listen.

"You see, Mac, I've always been a drifter and a no-good. Mostly because of curiosity and whiskey. I wanted to see the country and I wanted to read and I wanted to drink with people and to talk to them. So I learned how to operate a linotype machine. A linotyper can go to any city, pick up a few weeks' work, and then move on to another town. That's what I did, year after year. Outside of working hours I divided my time about equally between the bars and the public library."

"The library!" exclaimed the judge.

"Sure. I had a thirst for bourbon that was equaled only by a thirst for literature. That's how I got my moniker—they all call me the Professor. But this is no sob story. I am not one whom 'unmerciful disaster followed fast and followed faster.' Everything that has happened to me is nobody's fault but my own."

The big man paused. The judge was suddenly aware of a vast silence. No footsteps overhead, no voices below. Of course, that late on Sunday, there would be nobody upstairs in the courthouse except the night man on jail duty. But downstairs. . . .

"Are we the only people in the jail?" asked the judge.

The Professor nodded.

"By the way, why did they put me in with you? Why not a separate cell for each of us?"

"Traditional," replied the Professor. "Following precedent, no doubt, like the law. Although I must say that the jail business is mighty slow in Hartville on a Sunday."

"Result of sound law enforcement," murmured the judge.

"What was that?"

"Nothing," said the judge hastily. "Go on with your story."

"Well, what happened was that as I grew older I began to get bored with drifting. So when I landed in the *Blade* composing room in Kane City, I thought I'd see if I could stick it out; stay reasonably sober, work steady, keep the job. Well, I didn't do too well. They got to calling me Old Unreliable. Oh, I would have periodic lapses of sobriety, but 'beaded bubbles winking at the brim' I could not withstand. And then, Mac, I met a woman."

The big man gestured dramatically. "Oh, hers is not a face

to launch a thousand ships," he said. "She's a schoolteacher. What I found was something I had never found before—a woman who loved books, a woman who had a love for poetry and a profound respect for good prose. So I asked her to marry me. She said that if I'd promise to quit drinking she'd think about it. She told me to mull it over very carefully, and believe me, I did. I finally wrote her a letter saying yes, I would. And back came a letter from her saying yes, in that case, *she* would. Now, Mac, I want you to understand my position at that moment."

The Professor hunched his shoulders and pointed a wagging finger. "I was due to see her the next afternoon. That gave me one last chance to say farewell forever to John Barleycorn, and I can assure you that was no light project. Strenuous measures were called for. In the morning I would climb on the well-known wagon, but this night Bacchus would claim me for his own. And so, Mac, I proceeded to hang one on that would have been the envy of Commodus."

He grinned ruefully. "There's a joint halfway between Kane City and Hartville where I went to say, 'Bye, bye, bourbon.' This is what they tell me I did. They say I got in my car, drove it into Hartville at eighty miles an hour, almost sideswiped an ambulance, and almost ran down an old lady, went right through a man's yard and through his back fence and through another yard on the next street, and finally smashed into a tree. And when the police dragged me out of the wreck and asked me what I thought I was doing, I told them I was Ben-Hur."

He shook his head sadly. "Now, Mac, I ask you," he said, "can I expect that human icicle, that Bloodless Bentley, to understand *why* a man would go out and get that drunk because he was going to get married and stay sober ever after?"

The judge was silent. For some minutes nothing was said. It had been dark outdoors for a long time, and the single bulb of the cell gave out a dim, hard light.

"I've been thinking," the big man started up again, "that if I could just get out of here, I could somehow work it out. I could thumb a ride to some town where there's an office of the typographical union, where they know me, and I could borrow enough money to get so far away they wouldn't try to bring me back here. It would cost them too much, and after all, I didn't actually hurt anybody. Then I could send for my fair lady, and we'd get married. Indeed a 'consummation devoutly to be wished'! But no, no. . . ." His great shoulders shook.

"No, Bentley will give me ninety days at least, and take away my driver's license forever, and probably fine me to boot. I don't have any money to pay, so I'll be a jailbird and won't be able to get a job anywhere and, of course, the girl will never marry me then! I tell you, the prospect is almost enough to make me wonder whether it might not be worth while trying to escape."

"What!" exclaimed the judge.

"Let's consider it coolly, as an academic exercise in speculative thought," the Professor went on. "This building is pretty old. The former bastions of strength may have developed unsuspected weaknesses. For example, take a careful look at the ceiling beam that holds the upper ends of the bars on the front of this cell."

The judge looked up. Where the bars entered their sockets, the beam was split along its entire length.

"I have a suspicion," the Professor continued, "that beam is not only split, but rotten. I have an idea that a determined man might be able to pry those bars out."

The judge's heart gave a great leap. The big man drew close. "Listen," he said. "About midnight the night man watching the jail sneaks out for a cup of coffee. I know because I can hear the back door, at the head of the stairs, open and close. Then's our chance."

"But how could you get at those bars?" the judge was amazed to find himself saying.

"Lock your hands, and I'll climb up on your shoulders."

Up went the Professor. He pushed and probed. Down he came.

"Loose," he pronounced.

Break jail! The judge tingled with a sensation he had never before felt. He thought suddenly of the Count of Monte Cristo, and a queer elation seized him. He faced the Professor squarely. "See here, my friend," he said in a determined voice, "if we're going to attempt this, it must be done right. Just how would you propose to do it?"

"You boost me up," said the Professor. "I squeeze through and drop down on the outside. Then I reach my hands in through the bars and boost you up and you crawl through."

"O.K.," said the judge. "When we hear the back door click, we try it. *Then* what do we do?"

"Beat it, of course."

"Where to? They'll have searching parties out for us."

"We'll have to take our chances."

"Oh, no, we won't," said the judge. "I know this town, and you don't. If you want me to go along with you on this, you'll have to do exactly as I say, and no questions asked."

There was authority in that voice. The Professor stared at the judge in considerable surprise. "O.K., Mac," he agreed. "You're the boss."

So they waited, and listened. At last they heard the back door click. Five minutes later they were out in the yard, back of the jail.

"Follow me and keep quiet," ordered the judge.

He led the way—into a garage and through it into a lane, around the corner onto a side street, down that street to an alley, into a backyard and up a shrub-bordered driveway, through a vegetable garden and over a fence, and then into a dimly lit, tree-shaded street for several blocks. On a corner the judge halted.

"One block more," he said, "and we come to Ridge Street. That's a main street, and we have to cross it."

Cautiously they proceeded. Except for several cars quite a distance away, Ridge Street was empty. But then the high wail of a police siren split the air, and looking toward downtown they could see a flashing red light.

"We'll have to run for it!" said the judge. "Come on!"

And run they did—across the street into a yard, past the house, through a flower garden, onto a patch of grass, and then beyond it down a short steep hill overgrown with brush and brambles, landing in a wild crab-apple thicket. The yard was that of Oscar Begg. They had just passed under the black-walnut tree where the judge, that afternoon, had fallen into the clutches of the law.

"Lie down," commanded the judge.

They heard a police car roaring past. A second siren sounded, farther away.

"I want to explain to you," whispered the judge, "what we're going to do. We're in a little valley that runs behind a row of houses. There's a path up the valley, along the creek. The path is completely hidden by brush and trees. Up the path there's a house where the people are away. We're going to get in that house. Once inside, we're safe until we can figure out what to do next."

"Now wait a minute," the Professor put in. "I don't like the idea of breaking into somebody's home."

"We won't have to break in. The back door is unlocked. I've cased the joint." The judge was surprised at how easily the words came.

He led the way to the path in careful silence. They had just reached a spot where the creek widened into a cattail swamp when a ray of white light shot over their heads, and a voice said, "I doubt whether they'd be down here, but you never can tell."

A second shaft of light pierced the brush. "Might as well be sure," answered another voice.

"Into the ditch!" whispered the judge. "Flat on your face! Down under the weeds! Nose in the mud!"

Above them was a noisy thrashing about, the searchers playing their flashlights back and forth, up and down. But how could two dark humps, looking like rotten logs under the cattail shadows, have been suspected of being human beings?

How long, wondered the judge, how long. . . ? The October mud was cold, but he did not dare risk even a shiver. What were those stories he had read, as a boy, about escaped slaves hiding in bayou backwaters? Strange to be lying thus, a hunted thing, only a few rods away from that patch of purple asters, with their brown background of fallen autumn leaves, that had held him wondering that very afternoon. Strange that *he* would be fleeing.

Suddenly there rose before him, once again, the face of Mary Skoda, as she had sat in the courtroom, with her baby, and the face of John Skoda—thin, taut, pale, half defiant.

John Skoda. *He, too, had fled.* The four words seemed to echo through the cattail swamp.

At last the sweeps of the flashlights grew dimmer. The voices drew farther away.

"Come on, Professor," said the judge, and they picked their way out of the ditch. Within a matter of minutes they were at the back door of the judge's house. The judge opened the door, and in they walked. They were in the kitchen. The judge pressed a button, and on went the lights.

"For God's sake," began the Professor, in alarm.

"Relax," said the judge. "Turning on the lights will only mean to the neighbors that the folks who live here have come home. What would you say to a nice hot cup of coffee?"

The judge seemed to have an uncanny instinct as to the location of the coffee can and the coffee pot. In no time coffee was perking.

"So far, so good," said the Professor, "but where do we go from here?"

"I trust you realize," remarked the judge, "that we are now fugitives from the law? That if we're caught, we may be sent up for a long stretch?"

The Professor nodded.

"Well, now that I've gone this far, I might as well, as the

saying goes, be hanged for a sheep as a lamb. Professor, I
told you I had cased this place. I intend to take anything I
find in this house that I want. That will be robbery. That's
my risk. I don't think you want to be involved in that risk.
Therefore, I think, Professor, that you and I should part
company, and fast. But to get out of here, to make your get-
away, you are going to need money. You are going to need a
change of clothes. A description of you will have been sent
out as wearing no hat and a red sweater. So you stay here—
holler if a car should turn in the drive—and I'll take a look
around upstairs."

A few minutes later the judge came down, laden with an
assortment of hats, coats, and sweaters. A soft felt hat fitted
the Professor perfectly. They finally succeeded in stretching
a blue sweater over his bulging shoulders, and over that a
long, loose raincoat.

"Take a look at this," said the judge. Out of a pocket he
took a wallet, and out of it, a hundred dollars in bills. "Here,"
he said to the Professor. "That's your share."

"But I don't want to take stolen money!" protested the
Professor.

"Are you going to get away and marry the girl, or are you
going to spend half your life in jail?" asked the judge harshly.

The Professor slowly reached out his hand.

"Promise me only one thing—that you'll stay on the
wagon," said the judge.

"So help me God," the Professor said solemnly.

The judge put the bills in the Professor's big fist. "Now,"
said the judge, "walk out of here, down the drive, turn right,
and keep on walking to the second red light. That's where
a main east-and-west highway crosses Ridge Street. The

through buses stop at that corner. Get the first bus out of the county. Now get going!"

"Well, good-by, my friend, and good luck," said the Professor. "Remember, 'sweet are the uses of adversity.'"

It was with an emotion that was strange to him that the judge saw the big figure of the Professor disappear into the night.

At precisely nine o'clock the next morning, the Honorable Harrison Bentley took his place on the bench of the Court of Common Pleas.

He was indeed an imposing figure. His regular, chiseled features, the firm line of his jaw, his horn-rimmed glasses, his coal-black hair, combined to give an impression almost of majesty.

The courtroom was crowded. The jury sat expectantly. At the table were counsel for the prosecution and the defense. The reporter for the Hartville *Clarion* had pencil in hand. There was Mary Skoda with her baby, looking up with troubled eyes. And there sat the accused, John Skoda, thin, taut, pale, half defiant.

Everybody knew that John Skoda had killed Joe Kryslak. How would the judge charge the jury?

The judge began with a brief summation of the claims of the prosecution and the defense, then proceeded, with dry clarity, to define the degrees of guilt and the penalties attached thereto. The *Clarion* reporter began taking notes: with premeditation, first-degree murder, death; killing unpremeditated but in heat of passion, second-degree murder, life; blow not delivered with intent to kill, manslaughter first degree, minimum twenty years.

"I'll bet he gets life," the *Clarion* reporter whispered to his neighbor.

But then the judge paused, and with an unconscious gesture he took off his horn-rimmed glasses. He looked earnestly at the jury. "Now for a concluding point," he said, "which I wish to make very clear. Our statutes have been written, by trial and error, over the years. But that does not mean that the law should constitute a straitjacket. Justice is not a tyrant. The mandatory provisions of the law are, therefore, tempered by optional provisions which may be exercised, in varying degrees, by the trial judge and the jury."

Judge Bentley continued gravely. "A statute, by its very nature, cannot take cognizance of special situations or extenuating circumstances. But a jury can. In a trial such as this, on which hang the life and liberty of a man, the jury is permitted far more latitude than is generally realized."

The judge paused only a moment. "There is nothing in the law which prohibits this jury from bringing in a verdict of Not Guilty—if you choose to do. In that case, under the letter of the law, I shall be compelled to set the prisoner free. You may now retire to your room and search your souls."

"Well, I'll be damned!" said the reporter for the Hartville *Clarion*.

That night John Skoda, a free man, had dinner with his wife and baby.

Judge Bentley also had dinner with his wife, who had decided to come home earlier than she had planned.

"What did you do Sunday afternoon?" she asked.

"Just fooled around," he answered.

The newspaper lay on the chair. *Jail Breakers Roam Countryside,* said the headline. People were warned of two desperadoes: one a gigantic ruffian, the other a lunatic.

The judge's wife picked up the paper. "Why, Harrison," she said a moment later, "the paper says that crazy man claimed he was you!"

"It's amazing what can happen to a deranged mind," said the judge.

That night he went to bed early. His conscience was not easy. It would give him trouble, he knew, for many a day. But, just the same, deep within him was a sense of satisfaction, a feeling of the rightness of things. And across his consciousness, just before he fell asleep, flashed that pattern of wild asters, stars of purple on a background of brown autumn leaves.

ABOUT THE AUTHOR

Phyllis R. Fenner was born in Almond, New York, and for thirty-two years was the librarian of the Plandome Road School in Manhasset, New York. In 1955 she retired and made her permanent home in Manchester, Vermont. She holds degrees from Mount Holyoke College and from the Columbia Library School, and has traveled extensively throughout this country, Canada, Mexico, and Europe.

Miss Fenner's work has brought her in touch with library schools throughout the country; she has also done book reviewing, given lectures about children's books, and held story hours for children. In addition she is widely known for her many distinguished anthologies.